YORK LITERARY REVIEW 2023

YORK LITERARY REVIEW 2023

Edited by *Liliana Baldanza, Libby Bowler, Megan Gray, Emma Leask, Kummi Sandrasagren, Philip Treble, Cheyenne Uustal* and *Shannon Wibberley*

First published in 2023 by Lendal Press
an imprint of Valley Press
Woodend, The Crescent, Scarborough, YO11 2PW
lendalpress.com | valleypressuk.com

ISBN 978-1-915606-36-5
Cat. no. LP0018

A CIP record for this book is available from the British Library.

Contents

Foreword

'O, how wonderful is the human voice! It is indeed the organ of the soul. The intellect of man is enthroned visibly on his forehead and in his eye, and the heart of man is written on his countenance, but the soul, the soul reveals itself in the voice only.'
— Henry Wadsworth Longfellow, *Hyperion*, 1836

Voices transport us.

When I hear the twang of a Brummie accent I am taken home. Suddenly I am a kid, hanging out on street corners with my mates. *Alright, babs?* and I instantly remember my Uncle and his infamous house parties, reaching out and putting his arm around my Mother's shoulders. Those lost to us remembered through voices. Even though I say I have never had a Brummie accent, I still find it appearing in my voice when speaking to members of my family. I may have moved away, but my voice – my identity – is still there. Waiting underneath the surface. When it appears, I welcome it like an old friend.

A singer transports us into the dream-like world of memory. The tone. The passion. All delivered through the skilled (or sometimes unskilled) control of their voice. The voice is an instrument too, able to communicate something uncommunicable. Voices make us sad, happy, melancholic, angry, ecstatic, loved. They are singing just for you. Their voice is a bridge between their soul and yours. I remember the first gig I ever went to and feeling totally captivated by sound. I transcended through the power of voice. I have loved all forms of music ever since from country to heavy metal. In music, voice is a vital part of the whole mode of expression. Whether a calming folk melody or an industrial-fuelled growl, the power is the same.

Next to consider are the voices of history. York is full of these, whispering to you as you navigate the cobbles. The voices of the past echoing into the present to anyone whose ears are open. You turn down a snickelway and hear the sound of giggling children when none are in sight. York is a ghostly city, the voices of those long gone faintly present amongst the modern-day hum. However, avoid these past voices at your own cost! They warn us. *Don't repeat the mistakes of history!*

The voice is the vessel for knowledge. We learn by listening to people talk, by taking in their words and letting them sit within our minds. Brew, revolve, settle. We are moved to action by speech, by the political power of voice. Communication is key to our existence as social animals. We relish communication, the engagement with voice in its many forms. Voice extends beyond the vocal too. We do not need to hear voices to experience their greatness. Words on the page express voices too, and in this lies tremendous hope and responsibility.

Voice is the organ of the soul! Longfellow was right.

Welcome to the 2023 *York Literary Review*. The theme for this year is 'voices', chosen by the team of York St John University MA Publishing students tasked with producing the anthology. What a significant theme it was for them to pick! The world of the twenty-first century, awash with social media and 24-hour news reels, is bombarded by voices, all vying for attention, a colossal storm of endless communication. It is easy to get lost. To have your voice subsumed by countless others. The anthology's theme grew out of this concern but manifested in other wonderful ways too.

There was an inundation of submissions for this year's review. I think this reflects not only the openness of the chosen theme, but also a necessity to acknowledge forgotten or suppressed voices. There are figures from history whose stories have been untold. There are personal memoirs. There are voices within landscapes. There are ruminations on how voice connects to personal identity. This year's anthology contains creative writing of great power and significance. I congratulate the team and thank the contributors for giving us their voices. We are all the better for it!

Dr Rob O'Connor, York St John University
York, May 2023

Preface

Hello and welcome to the 2023 edition of the *York Literary Review*! Our theme for this year's review is 'voices'. Our writers have interpreted what the theme means to them, but what does it mean for our team?

The voice is a precious and purely individual aspect of our identity and sense of self. The very ethos of any publishing house is giving a voice through a poem, short story or fiction, to the masses, a voice that can be understood and deserves to be heard. The work that is produced expertly shows what the individuality of voices means to each person, from accents to memories to voices that have been silenced, each piece represents what it means to have and more importantly use a voice. *Liliana Baldanza*

In a time where more and more people are trying to get their voices heard, our theme seems more prevalent than ever. Voices not only reflects the simple, everyday conversations we have in our lives but also the bigger issues we aim to bring attention to. Our contributors have interpreted this year's theme in so many different and interesting ways, each being as important as the other. *Libby Bowler*

In a world filled with so much chaos, the only thing guaranteed to us is our voice. It is the sound of our humanity, building and sharing the emotions and experiences of the individual with one another. Our theme speaks volumes, capturing the pneuma of not just mortality, but the eternal being of the written word. *Megan Gray*

Using their voices, our authors can take the reader to places they may never have even imagined, evoking emotions that connects them to the story being told. Through the 'voices' theme our authors have also had the freedom to embody an entirely fictional voice through their imagination and creativity. *Emma Leask*

Voices are instruments that shape the world around us, changing the most objective statements to the most personal narratives. As a theme, it is something that resonates with everyone differently, yet equally as it relates not only to speech, but to communication as a whole. *Kummi Sandrasagren*

Our theme of 'voices' harnesses individual creative interpretation whether that is literal, opinion, reflection, or imagination. It encompasses and allows contributions from writers of any background and location. *Philip Treble*

The power a voice has cannot go unnoticed. All throughout history, it has been used as a form of expression and as a catalyst for change. Past voices are used to amplify the present as they create space for future ones to be heard. It is a theme that is as important today as ever, with each story, poem, or piece of nonfiction in this anthology showing the difference a voice or lack of voice can make. *Cheyenne Uustal*

Voices cannot be defined to one simple meaning, as our extremely talented authors have demonstrated. It has been interpreted in a magnitude of ways; allowing those of all identities to share their stories from wherever they are in life. This theme does not just express the power of one's voice but also the importance of individuality and freedom in the hope of making a change to the world we live in. *Shannon Wibberley*

We wanted the 2023 edition to be a bold, fresh take on the review, with a new contemporary feel reflected in our colourful cover. We are thrilled with the submissions we received and the fantastic work our authors have done when interpreting the concept of 'voices'. Every piece is unique in its take on the theme, each author using their own voices in such creative ways to explore what it means to have a voice to share.

York Literary Review Team

Here
Carl Alexandersson

at the end
                          of the day
            it's a
                  Sunday night
                                    at a gay bar
            in Birmingham
and
                  we become
                                          music
we have
                        and have
                                                not
                              heard before
our pressed chests
                              make out
a mass
            where
                              arms reach
                  for hands
and
                  feet find
            rhythms
                              like sunrises
find eyelids
                        you
            compliment
                              my t-shirt
but really
                  you're saying

look
            we're here

we are all
                              here.

english can't translate the heaviness of bearing a tongue that betrays you and reminds you of home

Shrien Alshabasy

My father's father shouted at him in Arabic
from balconies and store fronts
across soccer fields and chipped alleys

tainting,
the language that brings poets to their feet
and believers to their knees.

I'm sorry to make your pain
my poetry, baba
typical of a person who speaks english
to squeeze the shadow from a star,
the father from a son,

and call it art

you were a translator in Egypt
danced between French and German and Arabic
the same way you danced around a soccer ball

maybe it was this dancing that your father feared

knowing that an eldest son
who can move swiftly between words
between worlds
like an intentionally placed comma
can erase you, ~~he must've been so scared~~, in a moment.

and when you found the courage to leave your baba
and cross into *amreeka*, a country that sounds like
fenugreek,
fenugreek, the ancient Egyptians used to induce childbirth,
you birthed a new life in English, a language your father
could not find you in.

Between Aeaea and The Rocks of Scylla
Drew Boulton

She told you that you're breaking her heart
I don't know what she sounds like but I can imagine
Sickly sweet, but there's an edge that only you have heard
In my head, she says your name the same way you say hers
Like a secret that only exists between the two of you
I am being haunted by a voice I have never heard
Because there is no way of knowing if she is high pitched or low
If she talks at the speed of light or slow, longing
So I don't know how to make myself not sound like her
The girl whose voice I know echoes in your head
As she's telling you that she's been thinking about you lots
I hear my own voice saying I'm proud of you
Trying desperately to sound soft and warm in a way she
    might have
Begging you to see me in just a fraction of the way you see her
Because if I could have an inch of the love you give to her
I would take it and build a tower of adoration for you
Maybe my voice will never compare to the one before me
But I could love you enough for the both of us
If you would only let me

Subtitles

Carole Bromley

So, it's come to this.
No more lip-reading,
no more getting the gist
but missing the asides.

Now the film spools on,
my eyes flicking to the words,
missing the subtlety of expression,
the shrug, the gesture.

Only last week
the volume was on max
annoying the neighbours;
now I'm aware of the script,

its twists and turns
as if it was being written
before my eyes
Birdsong, he exhales, she sighs.

Polyglott
Cat Caie

My mother tongue is an interchangeable snake,
It threads through the needle,
Weaving soft velvet from English to Deutsch.
Wörte evade me in one language
But find me in the other.

Das ist what it's like to be zweisprachig.

What language follows me through my sleep, in my dreams
       and my thoughts?
What language do I think and speak in when I'm with you –
       or not?

I switch between two comforts
And find no sweet spot.
I switch between realities,
There's two me's that hold me up.

I'm my own liminality,
Neither one nor the other.
Not even two sides of the same coin.

A Family of Songbirds
Tinamarie Cox

You wanted to hear a familiar voice so badly
that you shoved your chords down my throat
and told me to sing, in perfect key, the notes you wrote.
But the tune wasn't quite yours either,
you had heard the song before,
long ago,
when someone else's voice
was planted painfully into your windpipe.

The Voice
Steve Denehan

the panic rises through him
swells of dark pressure
several times a day

he has fought against it often
but now
finds it to be
a kind of comfort

something to be welcomed
to give in to
a way of letting go

he is unsure of many things
the trivial now impossible
the faces surrounding him
having become
unfamiliar

there was a voice this morning
when he woke
the words were not important
only the resonance, the soft swaying rhythm

he listens to the voice
as he sits
in his armchair, and though
he finds it soothing
he is unsure
from where it emanates

part of him believing
that it comes
from within himself

part of him believing
that it comes
from a hidden corner of the universe

as if
there is a difference.

The Funeral is at One
Jeremy Dixon

'Cooking,' Emma announced, leaning back in her chair and smiling. 'You think?'

'Yep, stay at home dad, desperate to impress his breadwinning wife when she comes home from work.'

It was a game they played when they met for lunch on Tuesdays and Fridays, in the bookshop–coffee shop on Coney Street opposite the phone place. Emma chose it because it was handily placed between the estate agent's office where she let out city-centre flats, and the solicitor's office where Grace fielded emails and filed case notes. Grace agreed because she was addicted to the new book cocktail that filled the air: ink and glue and fresh pressed paper, and of the magic woven between the words within. The game had come later – an invention for which they both took the credit.

'That's a bit presumptuous,' Grace said, as she watched the balding young man in battered brown brogues, steer the blue canvas buggy across the shop floor, the wheels squeaking with newness, singing the tiny bundle inside to sleep.

'Not really, that's Kerry's husband, you know, from the travel agents on the corner of Lairgate. I met him at Lisa's thirtieth. He's nice enough, but a bit "new age" if you know what I mean.' She made the statement with a roll of her eyes, air-quotes and a wicked grin.

'Did he talk about cricket?' Grace asked, watching him walk past the cookbooks and thumb through a biography of Geoffrey Boycott.

'Bugger.'

Grace was wearing a black, halter neck dress and an emerald green silk scarf (which was Emma's favourite colour) wrapped loosely around her neck. She had a red rose pinned to the strap of her dress. It clashed with the scarf, but she didn't care because it was Emma's favourite flower. She was sipping a cappuccino and nibbled occasionally at a piece of lemon drizzle cake. She was too nervous to eat. There was a hole in her lately, one that lemon drizzle cake couldn't fill.

A woman with a caramel ponytail and pistachio eyes came over and hovered by their table, switching her weight nervously from side to side and coughing politely. She was holding a tray with a mug and a small white teapot, a camomile cloud curling from its spout. The latest thriller by Louise Penny was trapped under her arm. 'Excuse me,' she asked in a cigarette-stained voice, smiling at Grace and gesturing opposite, 'is this seat taken?'

'Yes,' Grace replied, lifting her mug with both hands and taking a sip.

'Only... I can't see.' The woman looked around, theatrically, awkwardly, stretching her neck.

'It's taken,' Grace repeated, glaring, returning her mug to the table with a dull clunk.

The woman frowned and shook her head, then slowly walked away.

Grace looked at Emma. She was sitting back in her chair, watching her through wide, maple-syrup coloured eyes that were so like her own, brows raised high on her forehead, lips nipped tightly together.

'What?' Grace asked.

'She could have been your new lunch buddy.'

Grace turned away, pretending to be distracted by a conversation about Orwell happening on a nearby table. She didn't want a new lunch buddy.

The lift pinged and a short, broad girl in her late teens bumbled out. She was wearing a pink flowered, badly fitting, lantern sleeved dress, black trainers and glasses. She had straight black hair as lacking in lustre as a piece of coal. A denim tote bag hung from her hand.

Grace chuckled and looked at Emma. 'Politics,' they said together and laughed.

~

Grace drains the final, lukewarm mouthful of her cappuccino and checks her watch. She must leave soon; she can't be late but she hasn't the courage to be early. She takes a couple of deep breaths, rises to her feet, takes her black woollen coat off the back of her chair and slips it on, collects her bag from the floor, heads over to the lift and presses the button.

The lift pings and the doors slide open. A tall woman with silver curls and a slight stoop walks out.

'Gardening,' Grace whispers. She waits for the argument, but there is only silence. Her stomach rolls and she chokes a little. She turns and looks back at the table she has just left – their table – at the cold hot chocolate, sunken marshmallows and the cream sagging, rolling down the side of the mug and pooling on the pine top – at the untouched piece of date and walnut flapjack on the plain white plate - and finally at the empty chair which her sister had been sitting in when she'd told her that she'd found a lump – where she'd tried to laugh it off, in that nervous, scared way, like when she did something wrong as a child.

Grace glances quickly around the room and wonders if she'll ever see it again. She thinks about the face she'll never see, the voice she'll never hear... the hole. She makes sure that she has tissues in her bag and that the reading is folded up and safely in her coat pocket – and enters the lift.

She checks her watch. The funeral is at one.

High Tea
Ron Hardwick

'How long is it since we had high tea together?' I ask.

'Last month.'

My old friend Joe and I are seated in the Westlea Hotel, one of the posher eateries in town. I have to whisper when I speak to him, lest anyone should overhear me.

'How is your scone?' asks Joe.

'Palatable,' I reply.

'They always are at the Westlea,' says Joe. 'Do you remember when we used to come here after playing tennis? We'd often have tea and a scone.'

'You were always a better tennis player than me.'

'It's all in the wrist action,' says Joe. 'You always had floppy wrists.'

I look around the dining-room. There are a dozen folk eating cream teas, most of them elderly. The woman on the table next to me is so interested in our conversation she almost has her elbow on my plate.

'The town's changed a lot since then,' I reflect, 'all these new houses being built on the outskirts. Soon you'll not be able to recognise the place.'

'Don't forget the shops closing,' says Joe.

'That's the internet,' I say, 'two clicks of a mouse. You don't have to move from your armchair.'

'Kiss of death for the shops, that,' says Joe.

'Do you remember the Co-op on the High Street?' I ask him.

Joe nods.

'My mother,' I say, 'could still remember her divvy number till the day she died.'

'As could most mothers,' remarks Joe.

'And the cashier,' I add, 'sat in a central office and sent your change down in a tube along some wires. That always fascinated me.'

'The Co-op had huge chunks of butter and cheese on the counter,' says Joe. 'They used to cut off what you needed, weigh it on an old-fashioned set of scales, and wrap it up in blue paper. None of this plastic packaging that's destroying the oceans.'

'You can hardly open some of these shrink-wrapped goods,' I say.

'Those were simpler times,' says Joe. 'The world's the poorer for all this disposable stuff. We never had any money, so we repaired everything that went wrong. We never threw anything away.'

'I know,' I reply, 'my dad made me a cart with planks of wood and four pram wheels. A bit of clothes line to steer with, a stick to use as a rudimentary brake that stopped you if you were lucky, and hours of fun on Huddleston Hill.'

'Kids these days don't know they're born,' says Joe. 'They sit behind games consoles, goggle-eyed, hardly ever venturing out the house.'

'We were never *in* the house,' I reply.

'On weekends, and holidays, my mother kicked me out straight after breakfast,' remarks Joe.

'Do you remember we used to play cricket on that narrow piece of land near the burn?' I ask him.

Joe nods his head.

'We learned to play straight,' I say, 'if you tried a cover-drive the ball would end up in the water. We couldn't afford to lose a ball. That burn was fast-flowing.'

'Filled in, now,' says Joe. 'That strip of land is someone's garden. Those big houses, they swallowed up what we thought was common land.'

'I suppose the town planners did a deal with the builders,' I say.

'Sounds like a brown envelope job to me,' replies Joe.

The waiter sidles up and asks us if we'd like more tea. I say 'yes' for both of us. He brings a silver teapot and lays it carefully on the table, as if it might spring up and bite him.

'Those were the days,' says Joe. 'You could buy a pack of three Player's Weights for eightpence. No-one bothered to check our ages. I was twelve when I bought my first pack from old Farley the Grocer. He was only too pleased to sell them to me. Times were hard.'

'You always were a heavy smoker,' I say.

'Never regretted it. I know what it does to your health, but I wanted to enjoy my life.'

'You did that. You married well, too.'

'Oh, my Clara. She was a queen,' says Joe, 'never had a bad word to say about anybody. Always had a smile on her face.'

'Pity she didn't bear you any children,' I say.

'My fault. Low sperm count, the quack said.'

'Doctor Morris?'

'Yes. Miserly old Scotsman with a heavy moustache and the manner of a chief mourner at a funeral.'

'He was my Uncle Jack's doctor,' I say, 'treated his chilblains well, so I'm told.'

'One of the old school,' remarks Joe, 'we were terrified of him as kids. They say the new doctor looks about thirteen and wears an open-necked shirt.'

'Doctor Morris would turn in his grave,' I say, 'if he knew that.'

I glance out of one of the big picture windows that front the hotel lawn. A magpie is busy searching for something to eat. It's bad luck to see a magpie on his own. His mate flits into view and I heave a sigh of relief.

'Same with the teachers,' I say, 'do you remember the geography master, Mr Gordon?'

'I certainly do. Wicked old beggar.'

'If someone disturbed him in class whilst he was at the board, he would pick up the blackboard rubber and hurl it at the offending pupil.'

'Normally Smithy,' says Joe.

'Yes. Smithy wasn't right in the head. They would say he had 'learning difficulties' these days. They would look out for him if he were at school now. The teachers weren't half cruel to him then.'

'Brought it on himself,' says Joe. 'Used to bring caterpillars in matchboxes to school and scare the girls half to death - threatening to put them down the front of their blouses.'

I break into a gurgling laugh, like water draining from a sink. Joe always had the knack of making people laugh.

The woman at the next table is whispering something to her companion, a stern-faced woman with grey hair.

'What do you suppose they're talking about?' I say, in a low voice.

'Oh, the usual rubbish, I expect,' says Joe, 'soap operas, the price of eggs, the length of last week's sermon, the headmaster having a fling with the school secretary, that type of thing.'

'You don't think they're talking about us?'

'Why should they?' says Joe. 'We've nothing to be ashamed of. They can mind their own business, if those two cackling hens *are* rabbiting on about us.'

I'm sure the stern woman hears Joe, for she gives us a look that would melt a glacier.

I look at my watch. It's four-thirty. Soon the sun will start to sink in the west and I will have to think about going home. If I'm honest, after my Linda died, I have found it a struggle to keep going, which is why I welcome these monthly teas with my old friend. It's hard, living in retirement on your own, waking up in an empty bed where once your comely wife lay beside you, and now you only have the radio for company. Loneliness and boredom are the two greatest threats to a long life, I think. My two have flown the nest, of course, one to Australia, the other to South Africa, but they do ring me from time to time, when they remember. I was thinking about getting a little dog, but I'm not walking so well these days and I'm frightened I wouldn't be able to exercise him properly.

'I suppose you'll be going back home soon?' says Joe, reading my thoughts. He's very perceptive.

'Yes. I've a casserole in the slow cooker.'

'Beef?'

'Chicken.'

'Chicken's no good,' says Joe, 'you need iron. You don't get iron from chicken. You get it from beef.'

'Beef's very expensive,' I reply, 'I've only got my pension. You have to make do.'

'You can't skimp on food,' says Joe, 'you need to keep your strength up.'

'It's a bit late for that,' I say, 'when you're eighty-three.'

Joe chuckles.

'You'd best drink your tea, then, before you go.'

I drain the white china cup with its gold rim and replace it on the saucer.

'This time next month, Joe?'

'Same time, same place,' says Joe.

We part and I walk out into a cold, bleak Market Street and head home to my little terraced house on Montague Road.

The stern-faced woman calls over the waiter. He almost genuflects as he approaches her table.

'That man who's just left has really annoyed me. He kept mumbling away whilst my friend and I were trying to have a conversation. Something ought to be done about him.'

'That's old Mr Simpson,' says the waiter. 'He comes here every month, regular as clockwork, and orders high tea.'

'He kept muttering to himself. It was very off-putting.'

'He doesn't think he's muttering to himself, madam. He thinks he's talking to an old friend.'

'Friend?'

'Joe Palfrey. Mr Simpson and he were in the army together. They served in Northern Ireland during the Troubles. Out on patrol one day, Mr Simpson saw Joe blown to pieces by an IRA bomb. It sort of disarranged his mind.'

Julia Vinograd
Mark Heathcote

When a poet of the poets is gone
a slow grieving process takes place:
People are thrown together – in honour of an unfamiliar name,
a flame, it trembles into being a star on a new horizon.
Julia Vinograd is such a star, her light shall-shine-perpetually
her humanity, a beacon, shall cross continents near and far.
Julia Vinograd, Day in Berkeley will live on in permanence
to the discovery of each new generation, glad of her existence
sad that her voice no longer narrates the joys of their
    splendid days.

The Killing Kind

Christina Hennemann

As I'm speeding on the N4 to Sligo, heading to my sunset
yoga at the beach, the trees bent

under fiery clouds, I see a Badger spreading over the asphalt,
on the edge of the white
line severing grey and green.

A neutral voice on the radio tells me that women's
wombs are being combed now in the States,
seeking for living crumbs in every egg,

while Wolves and Orangutans crumple
their stomachs into little balls of cosmic dust, sinking stars,

but the voice doesn't tell me that, it's just
in my head, like a hammer on the pit of a cherry.

And then they quickly move on
to the war that's raging in Europe. At home, my people

are scared again, *What if the bullets patter upon us next?*
Berlin isn't so far from Kyiv, hushed screams or roaring whispers.

I never cared for Berlin, but I like my Münster; the first settlers
called it Monstre, an honest name at least
for something built by humankind, its pretty bourgeoisie a shroud

for the unseeable, the stiff collars a pillar of
consensual myopia.

I pass a cemetery and think of all the Badgers,
Foxes, Martens and Deer that should be mourned

right here, or someplace, and that my car should be boasting
a black cross, this coffin.

Violence in Gaza, rising oil prices, inflation,
I'm going to freeze in the winter, they say,

yet here I am, spilling into the sunset, my seeing eyes,
my capable blood-pumping heart,

and I'm still not on the pill.

Dawn

Kenneth Hickey

At dawn blood stains the empty streets.
History haunts like a rabid ghost.
Bright echoes remain,
they're burning books again.
Unholy texts. Heretical hieroglyphics.
Words lose meaning,
discourse denied.
The experts in ivory towers will decide
who speaks and who doesn't.
The rest must listen.
They have a golden plan
for every man,
each mother's son.
And poets still dream,
bright seam on seam.
Imagination's wing,
there we sing,
beyond the touch of mortal men.

Oy Vey
Tyson Higel

Fumbling through life
in a world of verbal communication.
I try to speak, but am only able
to mumble and gurgle partial phrases:
half-truths of my expression,
never fully articulated.
And there lies my consternation.
It's the difficulty in participating,
trying to exchange pieces of my mind,
of my being;
my thoughts on the way I see things.
They get tied up within me,
unspoken for.
'So quiet.'
'No personality.'
'What a bore.'
Are these righteous fears
of what others see and think of me?
Or are they only fictitious, to be ignored?
My vocal cords are never direct
to the truth of what I want to say,
so is it far-fetched thinking
that my mind might, too, be indirect
to the truth of others' perceptions?
Oy vey.

The Monster in my Mouth
Iqbal Hussain

Dear God,

It's me! How are you? I'm fine.

My mum says it's rude to ask. But I know you'll understand. Can I have a new voice, please? Mine's broken.

∾

The youngest of six children, I was the only one with a stammer. It was as much a part of me as my brown eyes and long lashes, making itself known whenever I opened my mouth. It was an unwanted gift, my steadfast companion – like a shadow, but instead of being attached to my heels it lived in my throat. As with a shadow, which lengthened and shortened over the course of a day, the severity of my stammer ebbed and flowed depending on the situation. Sometimes it was just a hesitation or a minor stumble; at other times, it was a full-on blockage, leaving me red-faced with both anger and embarrassment and the listener equally uncomfortable.

With the hateful monster in my mouth, I faced a slew of anxiety each time I tried to talk. I spent my childhood in a world of enforced silence, with my lips sealed tight, my heart beating at double speed and my tongue in near-permanent paralysis.

The Glitch. That was the name I'd given my stammer. I visualised it as a long-legged spider in my throat, all spiky and sharp-edged, like something slashed into being by Zorro's sword. It lived inside me, sometimes coiled up in a pea-sized ball at the back of my mouth, but usually active and moving around inside my throat, as big as a crane fly. When fully extended, its hinged legs and fat, raisin body tickled and scratched my throat, causing me to trip up on my words. The harder I fought, the more The Glitch fought back, the glee evident in its wobbling, W-shaped mouth.

~

'For the role of Narrator, I have Javed, Mohammed, Asghar and' – Mrs Müller paused as though not believing her own clipboard – 'Iqbal?' Her purple-eyeshadowed gaze lingered on my face. 'Are you boys sure? There are a lot of lines to learn.' We all knew what she really meant: *there are a lot of words to say, Iqbal.*

I nodded. How could I not go for the part? Mother would be so proud of me!

Javed stumbled through his delivery. Mohammed was even more wooden. Asghar read at a galloping pace, not pausing for breath. Then it was my turn.

I got up. As did The Glitch, on legs as shaky as those of a new-born lamb, rubbing its pincer-sharp feet together. It had been thwarted earlier, when I'd spoken in unison during a comprehension task. Certain situations were out of reach of The Glitch, such as when I read aloud with others, sang, whispered or spoke in accents. Now, with all attention on me, it would show it still held dominion over me. Unlike me, The Glitch loved an audience.

I adjusted the microphone, my heart skittering as fast as Asghar's delivery. Thirty pairs of eyes followed me. My cheeks flushed. The paper shook in my hand. I checked the first line. Just fourteen words: 'Nearby, on a hillside overlooking the town, some shepherds were watching over their sheep.' Simple. But The Glitch was primed.

'N-N-Nearby, on a hills-s-s-s-...'

side – side – change it – choose another word – quick!

For all the words I couldn't say, I created double that amount in my head. Telegraphic-style thoughts pinged along at speed in a desperate attempt to get out of my verbal impasse.

'...hilltop, overl-l-l-...'

overlooking – looking – drop it

24

'...over the t-t-town, some sh-sh-sh-...'

*shepherds – oh god, there's no other word for them – quick –
think*

'...some men were w-w-w-...'

watching – looking

'...looking over their sh-sh-sh-...'

sheep – sheep – sheep – can I make them something else?

'...over their cattle.'

The class burst into laughter.

I tried to protest, but the words stuck in my mouth. Referring to
her clipboard, Mrs Müller said Mohammed would be the Narrator,
Javed and Asghar the kings, and me a shepherd. My humiliation
was complete. Not only had I lost out to a boy who read with all the
charm of a Speak & Spell, but I'd been given a non-speaking role.

~

Often, I went to bed in tears, reciting my *Kalimahs* and finishing
by entreating God to let me speak properly.

Whenever I suggested seeing the doctor, Mother stared at me
as though I'd asked to have my leg cut off. '*Puthar*, what is this silli-
ness?' she said, picking up a bramble rose and threading it through
her hair. 'Your grandfather was *thatha*, just like you.' I flinched at
the sound of the Punjabi word for 'stammerer', knowing I could
never repeat its tricky repeated syllables. 'As he got older, he lost it,
and so will you. Now, put the light on, my *gulab jamun.*'

'Please, just once,' I said, laying a hand on her arm.

'*Beta*, Dr Khan is a busy man. We don't want to waste his time.
How do these look?'

She cooed and sighed at her reflection in the dressing table
mirror. I made to voice my frustration at her not taking the problem seriously, but The Glitch was ready for me. The words froze
in my mouth. The more I tried to shout, the more they refused
to leave.

I let out a growl and punched the cushions off the sofa.

25

Mother jumped in alarm. '*Beta*, enough! I have not raised *jun-glee* children.'

A volcano raged inside me. I was a freak. I couldn't utter a word. I couldn't even scream without the sound splintering like an arrow made of soot. I ran out, slamming the door behind me.

Mother said I'd started stammering when I was a toddler. She blamed my love of Coca-Cola.

'You would grab the glass from my hand,' she said, picking up an imaginary vessel, 'and glug-glug-glug.' The cold drink had apparently agitated my tongue and disturbed my speech, not just for that greedy moment but for ever after.

I found this hard to believe. Wouldn't other children be affected? Yet I didn't know anyone else with a stammer – child or grown-up.

'But you let me drink C-C-C-...'

Seriously, why now? No point – give up – drop the word.

'...you know, even now. If it was that bad, w-w-w-wouldn't you stop me?'

Mother shook her head. '*Puthar*, why would I deny you anything? Hm, my *chandh ka tukra*?' She squeezed my cheeks and lavished me with kisses.

I pulled away. She couldn't fob me off with this 'piece of the moon' nonsense. I wanted answers. 'Why me? Why am I the only one to speak like... like... like...'

this – this – this – oh flip, how I hate the 'th' sound – well, don't say it – swallow it, like it isn't there – she won't hear the difference.

'...like 'is? Why not any of the others?' I meant my brothers and sisters.

'*Puthar*, you speak beautifully.'

I shot her a look.

'My bulbul, what is this *bakwaas*?' I was her 'nightingale', as I sang often and loudly. Having a melody supporting my words confused

The Glitch and meant I was blissfully fluent when belting out the latest Bollywood number. Mother held out her arms, her glass bangles sliding down. 'Come, no more silly-billy talk-shawk. Give me a hug, my sweet prince.'

I stood my ground. 'I'm not drinking any more C-C-C-...'

Coke – just say it – Coke – Coke – Coke – okay, try the second word.

'...Cola. Ever. Never again!'

An hour later, I was sprawled on the floor of my bedroom, absorbed in a *Just William*, scoffing Potato Puffs and sipping the Alpine pop man's finest Cola.

∿

The bus driver waved me on while continuing with his paperwork. With his attention elsewhere, I got my words out fine: 'Single to Audley Range.' Allowing myself a mental pat on the back, I got ready to hand over the fare.

Then the driver looked up and said: 'Sorry, pal, what was that?'

Just like that, my confidence shattered. With the driver's full gaze on me, The Glitch rattled into life and hooked its claws into my throat. My skin went clammy, my breath caught and I hissed like a snake in distress.

'S-S-S-S-...'

Single to Audley Range. Single. Single.

'S-S-S-...'

Oh God – he's looking at me – like I'm an idiot – pretend you've lost your money.

I dropped to the floor, scrabbling around, buying valuable seconds. I then got up quickly, hoping the act of rising would dislodge the word.

'S-S-S-S-...'

Oh no – people – behind me – quick – say something. Au-Au-Au-Au- Really? 'Au' is now a problem? Keep going – push the word out – push it!

'Au-Au-Au-Au-Au-AudleyRangeplease!'

The bus driver thrummed on the steering wheel. 'Audley, was that, cock?'

I nodded, not trusting myself to be able to say 'Yes'.

'What's the hold-up?' shouted someone in the queue behind me.

I lurched down the aisle and sank into my seat, my ears burning red.

~

In the evening, I'd be drained from the multiple conversations I'd had – the real, broken ones spoken aloud and the alternative, fluent ones in my head with the words I should have said.

I'd visualise an escalator, like the one on *The Generation Game*. Instead of cuddly toys and toasters, the prizes were words. I kept the 'easy' ones and got rid of the ones I knew caused problems. Each day, I dispatched hundreds, if not thousands, of words. Those I rejected got dumped through a trapdoor with a klaxon sound. On bad days, the pile under the trapdoor threatened to reach up to the conveyor belt and stop it completely.

The build-up to a potentially triggering event would start well before the incident. So, if I was reading a story in class on Wednesday, my anxiety would flare into life on Sunday evening. As D-Day approached, I'd find myself more and more lockjawed.

Like a chess player, I thought several moves ahead. I lived my life always a few seconds in the future. If I suspected a problem word on the horizon, I'd set my mind to finding a word I knew I could say. In a few seconds, I'd face the linguistic iceberg in my path, praying I'd chosen the correct word with which to circumvent it.

Some words were guaranteed to trip me up. Such as *today*, with its hard *t* and *d* in quick succession. If it began the sentence, it was game over; but if it came in the middle, I might be able to use the momentum from the words before it to soften its consonants.

Other words that left me floundering were equally innocuous: *didn't* (two hard *d*s), *just* (an explosive hard *j*), *remain* (my tongue would stick on the *r* and never reach the *m*) and *Mrs* (a deceptively small word, but it had missing vowels and a quick-switch middle *s* to a terminal *z*, all of which proved hard for my brain and tongue to process.).

Thanks to my love of reading, I had a large vocabulary. Like a walking-talking thesaurus, I swapped, dropped, or chopped words in the blink of an eye. I replaced *today* with *now*, omitted *very* completely and shortened *tomorrow* to *'morrow*. I may have lost shades of meaning with these high-speed replacements, but I was prepared to sacrifice nuance for fluency.

It took years to understand that the very things that were the source of my problem – words – were also my salvation. Like a homoeopath, I fought like with like, words with words.

~

What about today? Well, The Glitch is still there. Once a stammerer, always a stammerer. But my steadfast companion is older, as am I. Its days of high sport are over.

But, lest I get complacent, The Glitch can still take me by surprise. Like when I'm answering my phone. Or when asked to repeat myself. Or when making a presentation. Then I sense the cranking of its limbs. The brush and sway of its body as it hauls itself up. The metallic echo of its laughter as it digs its claws into my mouth. And the b-b-battle is on once m-m-m-m-... again.

They Will Put You on the Stand and Make You Face Your Abuser

Erin Hutchings

Your wings emerge a sudden –
ripping skin and dripping blood as they tear from your back,
wretched muscles convulsing as they burst forth –
and you scream in pain.

You look so deathly pale,
even as you grin like you've never felt more alive.
And, as you take off –
an icarus blasted across the horizon –
you laugh in a sickly, twisted fashion.

The blood surges down to the cobblestones,
and splatters a trail through to the dawn-light,
edging along the outline of the city walls.
And you stumble –
muscles not used to flight, to carrying your weight –
descending erratically back down to the bridge.

You're covered in blood like a child who has been playing in
      the fields and so I fuss over you like a mother,
licking my thumb to rub away the smear on your cheek.
You've somehow soaked your hair with it
and your twitching feathers keep flicking red all over the place.
It runs down, down, down,
staining the rocks and infecting the river.

And I know now they will hunt you
for the curse you seem to be –
torn dress, sharp nails, and blood streaking down your thighs.

Voice torn from the body.
So, I shall speak for you, and hold you close, and be
    your shield –

and I will hunt them back.

Murmuration Song
Jen If

Before murmuration,
the starlings gather.
Their chatter unfurls.

                  It lifts.

           Swoops.

                     Billows.

Suffuses the air,
soaks it.
Their voices etch the ripening sky,
til it's crackle-glazed.
Brambling notes
tumble down in swollen drops,
run greasy on the tongues
of the open-mouthed,
prick their tender skins,
overfill their flimsy lungs,
stuff and swell each bursting breast,
and
– just as the anointing peaks! –

Hush.

One intake of a hundred tiny breaths,
the heartbeat thrum of a thousand feathers,
into the full-blushed.

The Boleyn Haunting
L J Ireton

I see then, that I am to be silenced —

My letters, burnt language buckling
Inwards, inwards into a place
Where words don't exist.

Desire can't be undone. But
Denial dissipates the bonds
Of ink crosses on parchment —
Dancing black strokes
Transfuse
Into a substance
Of dust.

And in the blue light signing
I am unclaimed.
Under sentences of men,
Down through cold century floors,
Will memory hold its shape
Enough
In the telling
Of this?

I imagine a haunting.
Not of revenge —
But a ghosting of truth;
The voice of conscience
Is too soul-heavy
To be lost in consciousness.

There I will leave my voice —
Waiting beyond speech,
Latent and
Lingering.

What Does It Mean For Your Weekend?

Zeke Jarvis

'The police reported finding the body in two separate trash cans three blocks away from each other.'

'Is dinner ready?'

'Almost. The garlic bread could probably use another couple of minutes.'

'In culinary news, a pasta company will be discontinuing a popular shape. Stay tuned to find out which one.'

'Mom, did you wash my uniform?'

'It's in the wash right now. It'll be ready for tomorrow.'

'Thanks.'

'If you're one of the hundreds of people who have been impacted then contact our offices.'

'Will you have a little salad?'

'I guess.'

'It's not the end of the world to eat some vegetables.'

'I said 'I guess.'

'All right, all right.'

'The sale ends soon, hurry in!'

'Do you want to set the table?'

'Sure. Just plates, bowls, and forks?'

'Yep, that'll do.'

'The manufacturer that has been making the star-shaped pasta for decades has run into supply chain problems.'

'Leave tomatoes out of mine, please. I'll get heartburn.'

'Social media chef Ardith D'Amato has been using this pasta since she first started dating her now husband. As a farewell to the pasta, she's sharing her home recipe with us.'

'Do you want to get the dressings out of the fridge?'

'Glad to.'

'All right, it looks ready.'

'The trick is to add in a little extra parmesan cheese while it's still hot.'

'Can I go to Sammy's this weekend?'

'Friday or Saturday?'

'Sounds like a great dish. I'm sure everyone will miss it.'

'I don't know. Saturday, I guess. I think I just want to chill out on Friday.'

'On the political front, it looks like Congress has never been more divided. What does it mean for the economy?'

'Tell me about it. Come Friday after work, I'm switching from work clothes to sweatpants.'

'Oh, you're reserving that for Fridays all of a sudden?'

'Har dee har har.'

'The president called for unity at a Rose Garden ceremony.'

'Saturday should be fine, just make sure that you get your homework done Friday.'

'Ugh, I wanted to relax.'

'We cannot let these political divides tear our country apart.'

'You know what happens when you leave all of your work until Sunday.'

'That was like one time.'

'I believe that we can find common ground.'

'Your mom's right, though. Everyone gets grumpy when you leave everything until the last minute.'

'Oh my god.'

'Strong words, but will they bring the country together? Up next, a dog that can play the harmonica.'

'Okay okay, let's stop talking about it and sit down for dinner.'

'Good idea. Is that a dog playing the harmonica?'

'Sammy said that her cat can use the toilet now.'

'It... uses the toilet?'

'Does it flush?'

'It doesn't flush, but, yeah, I guess you put, like, a foil baking pan with some kitty litter right under the seat, and the cat gets used to just going in the toilet.'

'Breaking news: the potential outbreak that we've all heard about has happened, and it's even worse than we'd thought.'

'Does it wipe?'

'Cats don't wipe in the litterbox, honey.'

'Yeah, cats don't wipe in the litterbox.'

'Thousands of people have already fallen seriously ill, and because it shares symptoms with other illnesses, it's hard for experts to track the main sources of its outbreaks.'

'I guess that's true, but it's a little weird that cats have fur, and they're less dirty than people, who need to wipe, even though we don't have fur.'

'Can we not talk about this right before dinner?'

'Okay, okay.'

'Experts say to consult the CDC website for updated information and the best tips on how to stay safe.'

'Let's tuck in.'

'Let's hope that they find a cure for this horrible virus soon.'

'How is the pasta?'

'Really good, Mom.'

'Are you sure that you're not just trying to butter me up to get time over at Sammy's?'

'Mom.'

'I guess I just feel like, when you get a cat, you know the deal. You should expect that a litter box is part of the deal.'

'Dad.'

'Okay, okay.'

'Tom, given the breaking news, do we still have time for the hot air balloon festival images?'

'I'm not just saying it to say it, though. The pasta really is good, Mom.'

'I'll have to give the local forecast as viewers look at the images, but, if we can go forward without the weather map, then, yes, we can see the hot air balloons.'

'Thanks, honey. I appreciate it.'

'A cold front coming through. What does it mean for your weekend?'

And Another Thing! A Creative Writing Career

Emily Jayne

'girls are taught again and again that only certain appropriate, preapproved paths are available to them'
– Laura Bates, *Everyday Sexism*

I tend to describe my experience as *strange*. Especially when it comes to what is a 'preapproved path'. The Careers Woman at my secondary school pressed to me, and all the girls, that if we were good at maths and science then we should pursue engineering. I can still hear her talking to our form, 'There aren't enough female engineers.'

Even at 14 I appreciated what she was *trying* to do – making sure that we knew that *girls* could do anything, even be engineers! But when it was my turn to talk to her and I told her that I was interested in art, she said, 'Perfect!' – My stomach dropped as she followed her excitement with an explanation about how *engineering* is all about design, and architecture for buildings, and making sure planes can fly... (I don't think she understood me.)

Plus, our careers meetings were three kids at a time, so I had no back-up when she said one thing and the boys to my right were like, 'yeah, Emily you'd be good at that' – because to them I was (probably) just the nerd, not an aspiring triple threat.

And then, a few years later – having proved myself a patron of the arts: music, sketching, poetry – I decided to pursue a Creative Writing BA (Hons) degree. A friend of mine unthinkingly told me that that was *a waste*. As if my passion for the subject was unimportant, and because I had the grades to say I was just as good at biology as music, I should become a robot and do the sensible, responsible, *we need more women in science roles* thing.

My Mum did genetics and biochemistry at uni, got her BSc, MSc, PhD, got a job, got promoted, joined the British Toxicology

Society. She lectures and travels and is outstanding in her field. She is an amazing (*intimidating*) role model. Her career has taken off and she always has time for family. She is the one who has always told me, 'If you can work doing what you love, then do it'.

I learned early on that choice goes both ways – I was fortunate to have the doors open for me at every opportunity, but I can't say that I am *completely* grateful. When I needed recognition, (I was always told I was '*smart*' but) all I got was '*you're not smart enough*', since I chose creativity. I was made to feel as though, somehow, I was letting womankind down. When I graduated, had achieved the dream, and excelled at the path I chose to take, those memories force me to doubt.

Maybe I should have been more practical... My only older cousin studied marine biology and wants to explore the arctic someday. I could have studied environmental sciences and be working towards ways of combatting climate change.

After graduating I decided to take a break from uni and get a job. I've always known I wouldn't be a journalist or publicist on a full-time basis. My interests lie with storytelling, not production. I will leave those competitive industries to those who really hunger for them. My dream job has taken many forms over the years: author/illustrator (age 9), singer/songwriter (age 14), primary teacher (age 20), and now, almost at 23... lecturer? Maybe. If I continue studying.

I'd like to stay in education because the year when job hunting was my new thing, I was content – but not *really* happy. I was nervous enough about looking for work when I overheard my parents discussing what (on earth?!) I was doing. And I could hear my Dad's concern, his doubt. Of course, that's not a conversation that I was supposed to hear, and he would only ever support me to my face – but it showed me that I was still having to fight. To prove over and over again that I can make good. Solid. Sensible choices. I've been brought up as responsible and (I'm sorry Mum and Dad but I'm at the age now where) I know what's best – for me.

I might not get a job as one but, I am a writer. A writer with doubts. Like any artist really, told too many times: *you'll never make a living.* Because *all* I'm doing is making people *feel* things. I doubt my own abilities, because I like writing romances and (because I'm a woman) that happens to put me in a box labelled 'clichés'. And even though I'll turn my hand to anything – new content, style and genre, and am always learning how to uncover my own voice – I doubt it will ever be enough. But that will never be enough to stop me.

Maybe I should have gone into the sciences, worked towards saving the planet – what could I possibly do sitting here and scribbling? I'll just *waste* my talents away – fuelled by passion and the magic of creation, with the training and dedication to the cause of changing the world. One word, one line, one rhyme at a time.

It's great that what were once considered 'all male industries' are opening up opportunities for women but, can we please try to not swing the door round so it shuts on the other side? Just because I *can* be something – am finally *allowed* to be, does not mean it's for anyone else to decide. The final call is mine. So, if it wasn't clear: I won't be regretting my decision or shutting up about the *little* things. I will write about them all. Because (and this is key) after I've mic-dropped, walked off-stage to cheers and applause, I will always turn around and say, 'Oh! And another thing!'.

Dissecting the Past

Anita John

When talking with you, dear brother, on the phone,
the voice of our dead father slides into my ear,
presenting a third point of view. So, I press the mobile
closer until there's only your words and mine.
At my feet, the dog listens, then opens the door by herself,
letting that draught enter before the heavy rain falls
and I remember, after you left home, the small room
where you warmed baked beans on a camping stove,
ate them directly from the aluminium can, delicious as caviar.
Then the sky is suddenly pouring and the dog paces
uneasily about the room and I ask how much water
can spill from the roof's gutter before it breaks?
My ear throbs from too much listening, too much
pressing out the voices of the dead. Through the window,
white lupins suddenly shine like beacons of light,
then stillness, cool mist rising from the garden trampoline
and memories of us bouncing and tumbling through the air,
the way we shut out raised voices as if they weren't there.

Death Mask of Dante Gabriel Rossetti (1882)

Dana Knott

*'If I die suddenly at any moment, it is my special last wish that
my remains be burnt. Let no cast be taken on any account of my
face or head.'*

— D. G. Rossetti, April 30, 1876

How quickly the skin begins to cool
even as the last breath lingers above
the mourners, the doctor, the formatore
with his pot of grease. Those who draw
curtains, still pendulums, cover mirrors,
those who gather clothes to dye black
perform their tasks like sombre puppets.

How quickly the formatore anoints
the skin with the contents of his pot,
taking care to smooth into eyebrows
and beard with reverential touch.
The bedclothes smell of rotting pears
and troubled sleep. Solitary brain
cells spark like doomed fireflies.

The formatore pantomimes the rituals
of ancient Egyptian priests, layering
the face with linen strips and plaster,
smoothing surfaces with a lover's
familiarity. An intimate medium,
plaster captures both man and ghost,
resemblance and death's distortion.

The ghost of Rossetti's wife visited
him for two years until he closed
his third eye with chloral hydrate
and whisky. During a seance, he asked,
'Are you happy? Are you in heaven?'
But when he asked her, 'Will I see you
again?' she gave him no reply.

Death, Taxes and Karaoke
Grace Laidler

If you were to ask me where I am on a Saturday night, I will say the same thing every week: karaoke! I don't know what it is, but there's something so magical about being in a crowded bar with hundreds of other people, listening to someone butcher a UK Top Ten hit from the early 'oos.

And so, on a very cold November Saturday, after I swiftly reapplied my makeup, I pulled on my bulky puffer coat over the top of my black dress and tights, and headed out onto the misty streets of Newcastle. With considerable pace, I set off towards Frankie's Bar in the Bigg Market, which was conveniently only fifteen minutes from my flat. Or ten if you are sprinting to keep warm.

Now, as a self-proclaimed seasoned karaoke expert, I have found that it is best to arrive at around nine. The doors open at seven, with the karaoke itself not starting until eight, but everyone's still too sober then, so it doesn't get into full swing until nine. However, this is a bit of a gamble, as the list to sing will be *incredibly* long by nine, even on a so-called quieter night, so it's the luck of the draw, really.

I know. Karaoke is a minefield.

I arrived at Frankie's for quarter to nine, greeted by the bouncer, who asked how I was. I replied that I was good, but as he searched my bag, he did a double take at my face.

'You look like you've been crying,' he said. 'You alright?'

'Yeah,' I said, jovially. 'I just have a bad cold, that's all.'

His shrewd gaze told me that he was unconvinced, but he handed me my bag and bade me a nice night. After I paid the entry fee and got my hand stamped with a little microphone, I descended the stairs and opened the double doors.

Frankie's was very busy, packed even. Every table was taken, the bar queue was never-ending and there were several groups huddled like penguins to protect and defend 'their spot' on the floor.

I stood by the entrance to the bar, surveying the room. It was hard to see anyone in the dark purple haze, as the spotlights were aimed at the stage, where there was someone singing 'Valerie' (obviously). I simply exhaled.

Suddenly, from my left, I heard a familiar voice shout, 'Mollie! Mol!'

I turned to see my friend, June, sitting on the windowsill next to the stage with her boyfriend and a couple of flatmates. She was wearing an oversized jumper over her dress and holding a pint in each hand. I hurried over to her, making sure to not knock into the singer in my enthusiasm. I hugged June tightly, making the pints wobble dangerously. I took one from her and sat down.

'Hey, where's—' she began, but I cut across her quickly,

'—he had to go! He has football in the morning, so he wanted an early night.'

'Oh, okay,' June said tentatively. 'That's a shame.'

'Yeah, but it can't be helped.'

'I guess.'

June took a sip of her drink, then joined in her flatmates' conversation.

I checked my phone. No messages. No calls. I put it on 'Do Not Disturb' and took a big swig of my pint. I was there to enjoy myself.

All of the karaoke stereotypes were out in full force that evening. There were the first-timer girls, who were incredibly giddy when they attempted 'How Will I Know'. There was the girl who always takes it too seriously by picking an Adele song that showed off her vocal range, rather than fitting the party atmosphere. And there was the boy who made every song sound like he was doing a poor David Bowie impression. And the boy who ended 'Bad Romance' by doing the splits. And there were the hen parties that went through the entire 'Mamma Mia' soundtrack. And the idiot who sang the Christmas song in November and got rightfully booed off the stage. And, like always, there was the dynamic duo that sang slightly out-of-sync with the music and forgot the tune half-way through (although that's normally me and June).

From the sidelines, my friends and I clapped and whooped and cheered and sang-along with much gusto, fuelled by our never-ending stream of cheap alcohol.

'Next up,' said the host, at around half eleven, on pint number four. 'We have Lily singing "Your Song".'

A freckly girl with curly hair took the mic from him and started singing the song in a high-pitched voice. June and I waved our arms in time to the music. I was pretty far gone by this point, that warm buzz rushing straight to my head, seemingly draining all of the chaos inside of it. However, during the first chorus, I noticed something that made my stomach plummet.

The girl was singing to her boyfriend, who was stood near the stage. He was recording her on his phone, but he didn't look at the screen once. His gaze was fixed on her, with a small, loving smile stretched across his face. It was like they were the only two people in the room. We were all just extras in their rom-com.

Suddenly, I could feel a lump forming in my throat. I turned to June and blurted out, 'I'm going to the toilet!'

Without waiting for a reply, I hurtled out of the bar and up the stairs, then turned left into a toilet cubicle, bolting the door shut behind me.

I put the toilet lid down and sat on it, head in my hands. A few deep breaths, then, for the second time that day, I burst into tears.

Throughout the course of the night, I kept reiterating to myself that it was trivial to get upset over my boyfriend not wanting to come to karaoke with me. But I was tired of putting up a front. To be brutally honest, I was tired of it all.

The thing I have learnt about relationships is that they are like sharing a blanket. Each person has their own blanket knitted with their memories, interests, comforts, you name it. And it is so scary, yet so easy to just lift up our blankets to a person we love and say come on in. This is my blanket and I want you to feel its warmth.

But he wouldn't take my blanket. He would judge it, mock it, ridicule it. And for that, he was never warm; he was always icy, bitingly cold.

After a while, I managed to stop crying. I looked in the mirror, wiping my face. I had fully ruined my makeup this time. I'd done an alright job reapplying it before, but now it was a lost cause. Time to go home.

So, I left the toilets, feeling a bit guilty when looking at the huge queue my breakdown had created. I descended the stairs and entered the bar, looking to say goodbye to June. However, as my foot had only just crossed the threshold by a fraction, June rounded on me, yelling,

'It's you! It's you! It's your song!'

'What?' I said, completely dazed.

'"Go Your Own Way"!' You said last week that you wanted to do it, so I signed you up!'

'Oh, Christ, aye.'

June looked at me closely. 'Are you alright? You don't have to do it, they'll just move on.'

I looked at the host, who kept on calling my name, then back at June, who was holding onto my shoulders. Probably to stop me from swaying.

I could go home. I could go home, cry, lament, ring my boyfriend, tell him that he was right and karaoke was stupid anyway. Or I could sing. I could sing, stand in front of all those people, have the spotlight on me, and not know what the future held. I inhaled.

'I'll do it.'

With June holding onto my hand, I crossed over to the host, who handed me the mic. Another tip from this seasoned expert: don't put your mouth too close to the mic. God knows what is on it.

The lyrics were loaded onto the screen. The opening guitar riff started playing. With a deep breath, I began to sing.

During the song, I couldn't see the audience very well, as the dark lighting makes everyone look faceless. It made me feel like I was in my bedroom, dancing around with my headphones on, singing at the top of my lungs. But I didn't feel lonely. The audience sang along to my every word, elevating me more than any drop of alcohol could. And, Christ, did I mean every single word.

That was the magic of karaoke. We can feel the rush of performing a song that has a lot of emotional value to us, singing it as if we wrote it ourselves. And everyone in the audience will sing with us. They'll embrace the performance you're giving them. There's no judgement. No mockery. No ridicule. Just people, who have all felt the same pain and joy as the person on-stage. If there is a warmer feeling, I haven't discovered it yet.

After my performance, I went home. June wanted me to come clubbing, but my liver was crying out for me to stop.

So, for once, I actually listened to it.

I changed into my pyjamas and started to eat some leftover cake. As I was chewing the chocolate sponge and spilling crumbs all down my front, I knew that my life wasn't going to be the same anymore. But, amidst all of the chaos, the choices and the changes, there would always be three certainties in life: death, taxes and karaoke on a Saturday night.

Our Lass

Alan McKean

Our Lass were a bonnie lass,
Wi' a big, beaming smile.
She could coax t' sun out from behind t' clouds
At t' drop of a clog.

Nobbut seventeen year owd
When I first seed her,
Trundling t' setts t' t' mill on a cowd, wintry day,
Wakin' to a weak sun.

She'd a smile t' tempt angels,
And I thowt, *Aye, she'll do*
So I followed her t' see which shed she were in,
Champion, next t' mine.

I found t' courage t' ask
If she'd step out wi' me
An' bless me, she did! We courted fer two year
'til I asked her t' marry me.

I were floating o'er t' clouds
When she said she would.
Th'onny snag were t' cost, a couple o' weavers gerrin' wed
Might cost a bob or two.

It were a reet gradely do,
An' it set t' tone
Fer t' next lump o' years, bad times, good times
But always me an' Our Lass.

Wi' childer an' granchilder
We 'ad some times when belts had t' be tightened,
an' bombs, an' rations an' umpteen upheavals,
But through it all, it were still me an' Our Lass.

She were a bonnie lass,
Seventeen when I first met her,
Eighty-seven when she said goodbye,
Just me an' her,
Me an' Our Lass.

An' that's why I'm so lucky,
Y' see, I'm never lonely.
I've always got seventy years of mem'ries t' use up,
Seventy years of me and Our Lass.

Restoration of Voices
Debasish Mishra

Like the other vitals of a dead body,
the eyes, kidneys, lungs and the heart,
which are sustained and donated,
you can now preserve your voice

Singers are more in demand
after their death: their voices
are auctioned in opulent halls
that's how a deal is made
to buy melody with a babble

I have preserved my father's voice
and implanted it in my throat
I speak with his huskiness
and have become his version

I often gaze at the constellations
and converse with myself in dark
lonely nights, brushed by the skin
of his wrinkled crackling voice

And my poor mother thinks, my father
is still alive in flesh and bones
but afar, thanks to the secret
pact of the telephone and me

Voice

Quinn Murphy

At fourteen I learned,
That life's an unfair race.
The quiet voice is shouted down,
While the loudest make their case.

At fifteen I knew,
That my voice was mine to use,
I felt that what I said and how,
Was critical to choose.

At sixteen I realised,
That though on and on I spoke,
People didn't listen, and
My voice began to choke.

At seventeen I found,
There was far too much to say,
My voice felt very small,
Just a whisper in the fray.

Now, eighteen, I think,
Though my voice may be ignored,
I ought to speak on, anyway,
In case, in one, I strike a chord.

Date Night
E. R. Murray

'A cup of tea? Are you sure? There's a grand cocktail list...'

'I don't drink.'

'But you have a nip on special occasions, right? This is a special night. Here, have a look...'

He hands her the list.

'No. Not on special occasions either.'

'Ah.'

'What do you mean, ah?'

'You had a problem, like. Are you over it?'

She smiles at him, laughs softly. Touches her hand to his wrist.

'No.'

'You're still in rehab?'

'No! I never had a problem.'

'Ah.'

She pulls away. He takes her hand, covers it with both of his. She likes that his palms feel sticky. *A good sign*, she thinks. *Maybe this time, it'll work out.*

'Yer dad was an alcy, so?'

'No.'

'Yer ma?'

'No!'

'An uncle was it?'

She laughs again, louder this time. Painfully aware of the strain in her voice.

'No one! I've never had a problem, nor anyone in my family. I just decided one day that I didn't like drinking any more.'

'A fella then, Laura. I bet it was a fella.'

Her stomach knots and tightens. She sighs, crosses and un-crosses her legs. He notices how shapely they are.

'Look... can we ignore the fact that I want a cuppa? I'm having a nice time. Aren't you?'

'Sure am. It's just... Am I alright to have one though?'

'A cocktail?'

'A pint.'

'Of course!'

'It's not a deal breaker?'

'I said it was alright, didn't I?'

She catches the man on the next table watching and shuffles closer to her date.

'But you might be just trying to impress me. Act all easy going now, then as soon as I get into yer pants or a ring on yer finger, it'll change. It'll be all – no more pints for you, Jimmy. And then it'll be, take the kids here, take them there, dog on a leash kinda stuff.'

'Rings? Kids? You're jumping ahead a bit, aren't you?'

She's glad he's changed the subject. Since the accident, she hasn't told a soul. Never will. She stopped the drink, as penance. It was punishment enough.

'Yeah, well I don't mean it.'

'You don't want to get married or have kids?'

'Not this second.'

'Me neither, so relax, Jimmy. We're on the same page.'

He sighs out a deep breath, nods. The air is thick and awkward. *Say something*, she wills. *Say something to relieve the tension. Don't fuck it up this time.*

'So, you don't want to get in my pants then? You don't fancy me?'

'Of course I do.'

'Which?'

'The last one. I mean both. I mean – I dunno. You've got me all confused.'

'Look, why don't we start over. Get that pint and then we'll start afresh.'

'Sound...'

He returns with a tray. Teapot, teacup, milk, sugar, spoon. A pint of Murphy's. He places hers out in front of her, then takes a gulp of his own. She watches his neck bob up and down, imagining the smoky taste of it. Images she has tried to forget flood her mind unbidden; the thump, the body going down, the streetlights glaring as she sped away. *Penance.* She has made a promise and is going to stick to it.

'Jesus Christ, Laura!'

'What, Jimmy? Are you ok?'

'Yeah, it's just... he knocked you about, didn't he?'

'Who?'

'The fella that made you not want to drink.'

'There's no fella! Can't I just have a cup of tea without an interrogation?'

'Sure... it's just...'

'What?'

'Well, me ma says you shouldn't trust a non-drinker. They're always judgemental.'

'Yer ma drinks, I take it.'

'Sure. Just a drop of sherry at Christmas. A nip of brandy in her coffee. A spot of whiskey at the weekend.'

'Does she drink much coffee?'

'A few cups a day. Six or seven.'

'All with brandy?'

'Not all. But she's right though, isn't she? You're judging her.'

'No. I'm just interested.'

Thirsty, she thinks. I've never felt so thirsty.

'Interested – in my ma?'

'Yes. When I like a person, I want to know about their family.'

He puts his hand on her lap.

'This might be a bit forward but... do you want to come home with me, Laura?'

She grins. Stares into his eyes, hoping their blue is bright enough to erase the awfulness flooding her brain. *You should have stopped. Checked if they were alive.*

'Maybe.'

They lock fingers.

'It's nice you want to know about ma. You'll get to know her soon enough.'

'You're jumping ahead again.'

'Not really. I live with her.'

'What?!'

He snatches for his pint, knocks her tea over. She stands, wipes her skirt. *Penance.* He looks sorry, and all she has to do is sit back down and tell him it's OK. But how can she? *Penance.* She has no right to forgive anyone. His ma would see right through her in no time. *Penance.*

'I think we'll call it a night, Jimmy.'

She leaves, and Jimmy downs his pint. Turns to the fella on the next table. Rolls his eyes.

'High maintenance,' he says. 'I reckon I dodged a fucking bullet there.'

Where Your Heart Goes, There Your Feet Will Go
June O'Sullivan

Sahraa slides the items over the scanner, noting each beep, half listening to the chatter of the couple she's serving. Her stomach rumbles. It's half past ten, almost time for her break. Back in Kabul, at this time, she'd be in class. She can smell the art room; the sharp tang of the paints and turpentine, the bitter undertone of linseed oil, the musty paper soaking up watercolours.

Sahraa pulls her mind back to the present. There's nothing to be gained from dwelling on what could be, should be, or was. She is no longer a teacher of Fine Arts. That version of her is on pause. This version works the early shift in Aldi, in a waterlogged Irish town. Looking down the conveyor belt her heart sinks. Two bottles of white wine jostle. She waits for the woman to pause for breath so she can interrupt.

'They all get free buggies, you know!' The woman brushes her blonde hair back from her eyes as she reaches down for her reusable bags.

'Ah, it's desperate!' The man shakes his head. 'And all the homeless sleeping on the streets. It's not right.'

Sahraa surveys him. He is wearing a grey tracksuit but the generous piste of his stomach suggests little recent activity. She fights the urge to roll her eyes. She hears variations of this conversation every day.

'Ireland is full.'

'We should be looking after our own.'

She wants to tell them she would give anything to be back in her parents' home, surrounded by the people she loves.

'I'm sorry. I can't sell you alcohol until 12:30.'

The woman reddens. 'What? I thought the rule was 10:30.' She holds her phone screen for Sahraa to see the time. Her screensaver is the crest of the football team that Sahraa's son has just joined.

'I'm sorry. By law I am not permitted to sell alcohol before 12:30 on a Sunday.'

The man tuts. 'For fuck sake! That's nonsense. We'll have to come back again after our walk.' He glares at Sahraa as if she is the root of all inconvenience.

Sahraa shrugs. 'Cash or card?'

'Sorry love, I can't understand you.'

'Are you paying with cash or card?' Sahraa enunciates slowly.

Glaring, the woman waves her card in front of the machine. Sahraa sighs and presses the button to turn her light red, signalling her checkout closed. She edges out of her chair and heads for the break room.

She sits alone and slides out her mobile. No messages. Her stomach tightens. It's been four days now since she's heard from anyone at home. That might mean nothing she tells herself. No power to charge the phones. No money to buy credit. No signal.

Or it might mean everything.

She opens the news app and the screen floods with images so familiar their horror doesn't register any more.

Two men lifting a bloodied child onto a makeshift stretcher. A woman covering her face with her hands in front of a mound of rubble. An explosion, a market, an unknown number of victims, Dasht-e-Barchi, a Hazara neighbourhood, her people.

'Are you all set for Christmas, Sarah?'

Sahraa looks up. Bridget is smiling across the room at her, bright-eyed behind thick glasses. A friendly girl but, like all her co-workers, she has decided to call her Sarah. After the first few attempts to correct their pronunciation Sahraa conceded defeat. But she feels a twinge each time she answers to it.

'Will you not be thick?' Maureen elbows Bridget. 'Sure they don't do Christmas. They're Arabs.'

Sahraa bites her tongue and wonders, again, how it is that her education was cobbled together in a brief window of peace-time yet she knows more than these people?

'The boys are excited for it,' she answers. 'We will get them some things.'

Yesterday Sajjad brought home a colouring of the Nativity scene and instructions for the class Kris Kindle. She felt that twinge again.

Bridget and Maureen continue smiling into the deepening, awkward silence.

'Come on.' Maureen stands. 'We'll squeeze in a quick fag. Bye, Sarah.'

The break-room door swings shut on their giggles fading down the corridor. Sahraa punches in a quick message to her brother.

'Radin, are you all safe? Let me know please!'

~

Serge releases the letter from the typewriter and reads over it once more before placing it in the out-tray. Margaret, his personal secretary, will go to the post office when she gets back from lunch. She will look at him with pity in her eyes as she lifts the letter, just like she does every time he sends one.

Bohermore,
Galway,
10th Dec. 1939

Dear Jean,
    Many thanks for your letter. Please communicate urgently regarding the whereabouts of my wife, Sophie and my nine year old daughter, Rachel. I have had no news for many months.
    Serge Phillipson,
    M.D. 'Les Modes Modernes'

He is running out of places to send them to. He closes his eyes and tries to picture Sophie and Rachel. Happy, safe. Maybe ice-skating. Or reading together beside a warm fire. Last August, when they decided to return to France none of them realised the danger that was waiting. Tears leak out and Serge brushes them away. He stands, straightens his jacket, and heads for the factory floor.

~

La Normandie, décembre 1939

'I found some!' I call out to Stéphane, my voice muffled by the heavy snow weighing down the tree branches. My hands ache from the cold. Stéphane takes the bundle of twigs.

'These are wet, Rachel.'

'Everything is wet!'

All around me are frozen rocks and mud. We might be able to start a fire but I know it won't build up any warmth. Maman has already burned old wooden furniture from the cellar and is threatening to start in on the dining-chairs next. The wet is seeping in through my shoes and I can barely feel my feet. At least the chill distracts me from the hunger pains.

'Let's go back,' I say.

I lead the way slowly. Stéphane coughs all the way home.

Néris-les-Bains, juin 1940

Today I received a letter from Papa. I should have been happy but instead I cried. Oncle Henri says we might have to move again, further south, so that we are not caught and sent to the camps. I know we are lucky in many ways. Henri has money from the factory to help us all and we have a little garden where we've been growing vegetables. Ruth and Tante Ella have come to live with us awhile. Oncle Ernest must stay in Lisieux because he is German. Ruth and I pray every night that we will see our Papas soon. I like to imagine mine, making beautiful chapeaux in the factory in Galway. I wonder if there are other Jewish people there.

There have been no more letters from Papa. He doesn't even know that we have moved again. This time to la zone libre. Ruth and I hike in the mountains and look for blueberries. We can see into Spain! We could just walk over the border to safety. But we cannot. Grandmère is too old for the journey and we cannot leave her here alone. Henri and Stéphane have gone to Cannes. The mountain air was bad for Henri's asthma. I miss Stéphane. I miss everyone.

I thunder down the street, my wooden shoes ricocheting off the path. I am afraid. I shouldn't be making so much noise and I am running towards danger. I skid to a stop at the schoolyard. It is crowded and I scan the heads. In there, somewhere, among the hastily packed bags and distress are my Tante Ella, her husband Ernest who has recently returned, and ma chère amie, Ruth. The air is filled with fumes from the buses and the shouts of the police. The crowd is being herded onto the buses, packed tight. A figure breaks from the crowd and I see that it is Ruth. I stand with my toes gripping the narrow wall so I can lean over the railing to grab her hand. Hot tears flow down my cheeks as we shout over each other.

'Goodbye, my friend.'

'I love you!'

She is pulled back into the crowd and I fall to the ground. Someone is gripping my elbow. It is Tante Choura, her face raw with grief. Her husband, Oncle Robert, is being loaded onto the bus. Anyone who was not present in France before 1933 is to be sent away, deported. Our life is governed by these arbitrary rules. Who will it be next time?

Nice, septembre 1943

Maman is rubbing at my face with her coat sleeve, issuing final words of advice. She is saying that I must always wash my hands with warm water. This is important, somehow. I hear her words 'l'eau chaude' and I wonder has she forgotten? We are no longer the type of people who can depend on having hot water. Stéphane kisses her on the cheek.

'Goodbye Tante Sophie. I will take good care of Rachel I promise.'

He pulls me towards the train. Our little group has to split up for our safety. I watch my mother's face disappearing out of view on the platform. I am the one who is moving but it feels like she is reversing out of my life. It is her birthday in December. I resolve to save up my chocolate rations and send them to her.

St Etienne-de-St Geoirs, juillet 1944

'Jacqueline!'

It takes a beat for me to realise that I am being addressed. I have not been Rachel since January. For my safety I am now Jacqueline, a Catholic girl. There is no longer a Rachel, just as there is no longer a Sophie. Maman was deported in January and has not been heard from since.

The rumble of engines makes me look up from the well. A young, tanned soldier is standing beside his truck. He is smiling. He pulls off his boots and groans as he peels stiff socks from his feet. He hands them to me and I wash them in the well. While they dry he tells me about Canada. He gives me chocolate. I cannot eat it. We have been liberated.

Dublin, June 1945

A steel grey sea, teeming with jellyfish, chops at the boat as we arrive into the harbour. I disembark and walk towards my father. He is holding a bouquet of small, pink roses. For his small daughter, Rachel. But I am taller than him now. It has been years since we last met. In that time I have gathered wood for warmth, I have felt hunger, I have been hunted like an animal, I have said goodbye to people I love, I have lost people I love without saying goodbye. I am Rachel. I am French. I am Jewish. And now, it seems, I am to be Irish.

˷

Sahraa turns onto her side, the thin mattress poking springs into her hip. Outside, on the street, two men are shouting as they leave the pub. She is used to city noise, but this is not her city. She checks her phone again. Still no messages.

She puts it on the locker, on top of the pages that have kept her from sleep.

'Form 8 – For Naturalisation As An Irish Citizen.'

It will be difficult but maybe this is how she can bring her family here, to safety.

She is Sahraa. She is Afghan. She is Hazara.

And now, maybe, Irish.

Look Who's Come to Dinner
Briá Purdy

I wonder if she will arrive on Julien's motorcycle, the one which all those years ago sped Anne away from her prison cell to freedom, to love's sweet voice, and, all these years later, to me. I re-read Patti Smith's opening essay while I wait for Albertine to arrive. I use my elbow to turn the splattered page, stirring the ragu with a wooden spoon which balances divinely, precariously, on my chin.

It is seven minutes past eight. Albertine is late. I dump more oregano into the sauce, now deepest red and hissing at the sudden departure from subtly, that delectable *je ne sais quoi*. I have overdone it with my haste. Jittery, nerves have got the better of me. Now we shall all know exactly what it is: a profusion of oregano, too much balsamic, not enough garlic. I combat my nervousness with salt and a cheap merlot, which has been sitting, opened, lamely teased, on my bedside table for the past three nights. An acerbic blasphemy. I can't do much about that now. Albertine's luminous eyes lead me back and I grin with anticipation, and briefly consider changing my blouse. I want her to take me seriously. I need her to tell me all she can remember about her life.

Albertine is fashionably late. I forget to feel put out, irritated, raging over the pasta being way past *al dente* by now, but what can I do? She arrives at my door entirely herself, and I am excited all over again. Not 50 years postmortem, and Albertine's eyes still glimmer as if she has just seen something racing across the opaque room from the corner of her eye. Something delightful and perhaps a little sad. I wonder if she is a person prone to melancholy as I ask to take her coat. I realise too late that she is not in fact wearing a coat. Her bare shoulders smile at me knowingly.

'How very Parisian,' she says to me with a wink, waltzing on in, despite the state of her ankle, dressed in a thick white cast.

I remark enthusiastically upon her injury, the broken talus bone, *l'astragale cassé*: that precise and illusive bone located in the ankle. I tell her that I had never even heard of it – didn't even know the French for ankle (*la cheville*), before I read her 1964 novel of the same name, *Astragal*. A-stra-gal. Until this very moment I had often wondered exactly how autobiographical the 'semi-autobiographical' novel was. *Is*. It is very much still alive, despite the unaltered dead state of its writer.

I suppose this is my answer: Albertine, sitting on my sparse kitchen counter and propping her ankle, the precious *astragal*, up onto the kitchen sink. She is thirty years old, as she was when she died in 1967, just three years after the publication of *Astragal*. She is framed by the view, the skyline breaching the river. And my view is framed by her. Albertine appears in black and white, like an old film star. Only, she is not the leading role. Her beauty is beyond the myopic gaze of the camera. Her boldness lies in her writing. All I will say of her physical appearance is that it was most intriguing, and not at all unpleasant.

I decide, foolishly, to open with flattery. I gush with sordid enthusiasm about how good she looks after all this time. I don't mention the kidney surgery, worried it would still be a sore spot. I tell her how I loved her book, about how I loved Anne and Julien, the intensity with which she wrote such characters, such scattered plots detailing the ravaging of human emotion. The sore spoils of love are as clear to our young narrator as the broken lines of her ankle on the chalkboard X-ray.

Albertine lights up as we sit down to the dinner I have massacred. She does not ask, and I do not protest; the greyish haze of smoke will perhaps distract from the overcooked spaghetti, which dissolves in my mouth. Albertine doesn't seem to mind. Her interest vacillates, right hand lifting the cigarette to her pink lips, left hand lifting a twisted fork to that same impossible, smokey space. Her teeth flash red as she grins, wiggling her eyebrows in such a malevolent way that I am convinced that she is just another character from her novel.

'Paris was my gleaming Valhalla,' she says when I ask her about the city, about her relation to the place she ran to after escaping from a four year stint in Fresnes. 'Just like Anne I ditched that place' – she is referring to the penitentiary – 'as quick as a dog. Julien, Emilienne – all on my way to that great sparkling place. How I adore Paris! What little I lived of it was...'

Expensive? I say, hoping to amuse.

'Read my diaries, and you will know. Anne recovered there, while I was caught. Life is funny like that, isn't it? Anyway, I died – as you know – in Montpellier. With Julien, of course.'

You must have been quite the pair, I say, seeing them both speeding away on the motorcycle, Bonnie and Clyde in leather. Far more dangerous and outrageously beautiful. I tell her this last bit. I want to see her reaction.

She smiles tightly and I am reminded, shockingly, suddenly, of her death; her prostitution; her time locked away, these small, constant abuses battering her sails. All the same, she was strong. She rallied against such rotten dealings.

A success, undoubtedly. Her novels were bestsellers – La Cavale even won the Prix des Quatre Juries in 1966.

'Ah,' she interrupts, that sparkle at it again, glinting away in her unfettered gaze. 'Literary success is not the end goal. If, after all, all you require is to be known and to have commercial success, why not write, as any old man can, one of those true crime stories? Why even bother to define such a world, so close as it is to your own reality – if only to offer it up, part and sum, a pig's head on an ugly platter, to be devoured by readers who simply desire a fast moving narrative and believable motive?'

She smiles gently. Like a school teacher correcting a child, not wanting to discourage idiocy, merely seeking to redefine it.

'But you flatter me. I am no good at taking compliments. They make me break out in hives – only worse! My skin mutates into this awful stretched animal hide! My head will grow to twice its regular size!'

I think of the writers who have come before her. So many who, consciously or otherwise, are following in her footsteps. The literary tradition of 'auto-fiction'. The distilling of one's life into fictitious bounds. Misshaping, misdirecting, evading the pinning down of such inane questions— is this really you in here, on page 24? Are these 'characters' entirely constructed from imagination, or does a deeper excavation reveal concrete bones, the lives of those who truly lived? And ultimately, most irritatingly beside the point: does it add to, or diminish, a work of fiction, to wonder if its basis is in reality, here in *my* world?

I can't help myself. The three-day old wine is getting to me. It tastes foul. The grapes have turned mean with too much exposure, too much time spent at my bedside, repenting for past lives. I ask her what makes a writer. If the *writerly persona* is important, and if it increases or diminishes the writing itself?

Albertine seems tired. Her plate is empty and so she stands, limps over to the stove top and goes fishing in the depths of the pan. Spaghetti clings to her open mouth as she talks. It is hard to decipher the words, for she seems to be propelling herself tirelessly, frantically; stuck on this one, indescribable train of thought and muttering through minefields of dripping sauce.

The overall gist: she does not care either way. It was interesting, she conceded, to consider this in an abstract sense. But it was ultimately a kafkaesque debate. To recount the past liberates the teller, but the reader may infer, or impress onto such tales, whatever they wish. The writer may be plucked from obscurity, if needs be. Or she may remain the final, unknowable character. A writer can intend all they like (at this, she smiles fallaciously, and I wonder if she truly believes the things she is saying, or if she is simply teasing. Either way, I am enthralled.) but behind the page lies an equally unknowable reader. Theirs is the final say. For you, the writer, have already penned those final, aching words; they can never be taken back. That is all to be said on the matter. And yet the reader may take those words as the jumping off point, the diving board from which to hurtle back into those icy depths; coaxing out from the murkiness within, unspooling and unravelling all you have intended with that naive hand of yours.

'I was just a girl who escaped from prison on the back of a motorcycle with a man whom I loved. I have known happiness. I have met sadness many times. My past pleases me and I wouldn't change it for the world; to regret is to deny... and I hold my head so high, that sometimes I have cramps. There is life, and I write it so. Intent is forgotten, in the end. Anne is a delinquent, a *criminelle*; a girl seeking refuge, a girl in love. Maybe I, too, have been all of these things. Maybe my writing is because of, or in spite of it, who's to say?'

Albertine Sarrazin's short life may be adroitly compressed into a series of tragedies: maternal abandonment in her birth country of Algiers, revolt against her adoptive parents; victim of rape, imprisonment, prostitution; and then escape, freedom, love, writing, and finally, cruelly, that final tragedy, death. But death was far from the end for my Albertine. Death becomes her. It allows me to cook her a sub-par dinner in my imaginary seventh-floor flat in the sixième arrondissement. She invokes the rebellious spirit, literary revolt, irreverent femininity, sex, queer-identity, la Querelle des Femmes. And then, of course: freedom, pure and simple.

Albertine the Rebel looks up at me from the pan. She smacks her lips and her glasses are all fogged. Her luminous eyes are denied to me, covered in ash, in red splatters of tomato which dry like paint, and I get the feeling that this is how she wants it to be.

'Thanks for the dinner,' she says, licking her lips.

Umbrella Term

S. Reeson

I am not a term, fixed
for your entertainment. Value can
never be defined, as regard, in the cognition
as only something you're allowed alone. I see, deserve
everything presented within beauty, yet I am in reserve. You
extend each metaphor, forms observed. Here we both are

unable to commence relationships without conjunction, part
pointless speech, clause, as definition. We are an umbrella,
under which a thing, summarily becomes nothing
shielded from a confluence of truth and love
fixed, not yet a term.

I tried to open, but
you forced me;
closed.

Middle-Class Epiphanies
Bill Richardson

i.m. Kevin Higgins, Poet

A voice is echoing down the street;
Kevin, is it yours?
It's murmuring about a homeless man
with watery eyes and lanky hair,
and we can smell the humour off his breath.
It quivers when it speaks of millionaires,
and when we peep beneath the rug
to find out who they think they are,
their faces, like a priest's,
are dimly featured visages of fear.

That voice that echoes down the street;
Kevin, is it yours?
It says that our iniquities
are lurking round the corner
like some foxes waiting for the kill,
and our brand-new skirts and chinos
are pasting labels on the shield we wear,
while you, our *crazy leftie*,
keep reminding us of who we used to be.

That voice still echoes down our street;
Kevin, is it yours?
It says they're tearing down the murals
you used to paint when anger took a hold,
and shiny cars with number plates to die for
are hinting that they've laid a claim
to our respectability,

while sneaky cats in worn-out fur
are making off with all that we hold dear.

Now down the street that voice is hoarse;
Kevin, is it you?
Is it denouncing all the lies
so people we don't meet
can come to live, more or less,
the length of time the middle classes
take to wrap epiphanies
around the hole inside our heads?
The voice is swelling like an ocean:
we know it's yours – the waves it makes keep churning,
and the truth they tell shall never be erased.

That Soothing Old Irish Air
JY Saville

Jean could hear the singing Irishman as she walked uphill from the bus stop. She'd christened him Frank, though she couldn't have said why, and since she never spoke of him to anyone, it didn't matter.

'Hab-er-neeel,' he sang in a swelling baritone that never failed to lift Jean's spirits, and she stopped a moment before turning down the street to her office to let the early morning music wash over her.

Jean's father had for the first few years of his life an Irish grandmother. This had left both him and, later, Jean with an attachment to the 'old country' unshaken by the thought of how eager the grandmother had been to leave. Not for the first time, Jean wished she'd passed down the language instead of her blue eyes, a milk jug, and a garbled tale of an ancestor hanged for horse theft.

As she hung up her coat, Jean's colleague called her over: 'Come and meet the new intern.'

There was a girl leaning against her desk, dyed black hair in a 1940s style, leggings and a nose-ring. She'd forgotten they were hosting a student for a couple of weeks and she hoped she didn't have to play nursemaid; she wasn't used to young people. Fifty-three and childless, Jean had somehow managed to be surrounded by childless friends and cousins as well; some intentionally, some leaving it too late, some never finding the right man. Jean had found the right man but he was married to someone else and preferred to stay that way.

'This is Niamh,' said Jean's colleague. 'She's from Connemara.'

'Oh lovely, like the horses,' said Jean. 'Can you speak Irish?'

'I'm not some exotic specimen.'

'Oh no,' said Jean. 'I didn't mean-'

'Yes, I speak a funny language like a proper immigrant,' said Niamh.

Jean's colleague cleared his throat but Jean only nodded and looked at the floor.

At lunchtime she took Niamh with her to pick up the regular order of sandwiches. To Jean's delight they turned a corner and came upon Frank, sharing a lilting air with the pigeons down a back street.

'What's he singing about?' asked Jean.

'How should I know?'

'You're Irish.'

'What, you think we're all drunkards as well, is that it?'

Again Jean was upturned by misunderstanding.

'You understand the language, I mean.'

'That?' demanded Niamh. 'That's not Irish. He's just a sad old man spouting gibberish.'

Her nose-ring glinted as she sneered at Frank wending his way around bags of rubbish from the nearby shops.

'Ee-tern-ya,' he ended the verse on.

'Latin,' said Jean. 'It might be a hymn in Latin.'

Niamh gave a snort and a look of disbelief. Frank drew a deep breath, readying himself for the next verse or the next song, but Jean couldn't stay to hear it. She put her hand on Niamh's elbow and hurried her out onto the main road.

Thoughts of a Tabebuia Tree
Nileena Sunil

Humans think they know all about us trees. But the truth is, they know very little.

They believe that we are static beings that lead idle lives. They believe we cannot think, feel or interact with each other. That cannot be farther from the truth. We have minds as sharp as the best of them, we have thoughts and feelings and emotions. We can communicate with each other telepathically over distances large and small, though we aren't usually as chatty as the humans as we prefer to stand and observe. But that doesn't mean we don't enjoy the pleasure of conversation.

The other day, I had a conversation with one of my kin in a far-off land, a place the humans call El Salvador. She talked about the bloodshed she had witnessed a few decades ago (an exceedingly short span of time for us trees). That is one of the many things about humans that remains inscrutable to us. We would never dream of doing anything that would cause pain to a fellow tree... or any living creature. Yet, humans don't seem to have such qualms. You can never tell with them, if they'd strike a blow against a tree... or against a fellow human.

I have been fortunate enough to not witness such bloodshed. I lead a peaceful life in this park surrounded by numerous trees. Humans often come here to relax, walk around, and spend time with us trees. Some of them bring dogs along and take them for walks. Small humans run around and play games. Some humans bring food and eat under our shade. Many of them are fascinated by me and my kin, and spend time taking photographs of our pink flowers. 'Cherry blossoms', they call them, even though that is technically not the name, even in the language of the humans. I've spoken to cherry blossom trees all the way in the land the humans call Japan. They are pleasant enough but they are not the same as us Tabebuia.

I often wonder what life would have been like if I, like my ancestors and much of my kin, lived in South or Central America. If the British had never brought us to India. I imagined I'd be surrounded by trees of different kinds. Animals and humans too The humans would probably look different and speak different languages. But I believe on some level, humans are all the same. Sometimes brilliant, sometimes cruel, and often incomprehensible to us trees.

Today I have no plans to talk to other trees. I don't want to watch the humans either. All I want to do is watch the setting sun. I feel really fortunate to be in a place where I get a clear view of the beautiful orange rays. As I watch the sunset, I pity my kin in the city, outside the park. They don't get half of the view amidst the hustle and bustle of the city.

Ich liebe dich

Karoline Tübben

'I just know,' Ian presses.

'But how?' My volume attracts dirty looks from the table next to us. The two guys sitting across from each other look exactly the same, hipsters with long hair that hasn't been washed in a month, striped T-shirt and tortoiseshell glasses. I narrow my eyes at them, barely resisting the spiteful urge to stick my tongue out. As if they're discussing the future of world peace over there. Ian smiles at them apologetically.

'I do, okay? I just do. I can't explain it.' He glances out the window next to us where there's a couple walking hand-in-hand with their terrier. When he looks back at me, I know what he's thinking. It's not that he can't explain it, it's that I wouldn't get it. Maybe if I'd had a relationship, I would.

'Look,' he tries, the word coming weakly out of his lips with a sigh. 'She doesn't talk much. You know her. She's more the broody type but the way she reaches for my pinkie when we walk through a crowd or how she brings my favourite smoothie when we meet up in the morning after my night shifts, those things show me she cares. She doesn't need to tell me.'

'Okay then,' I shrug. 'If you're happy, I'm happy.'

~

When I get home from the café, the house is empty, no cars in the garage. The dogs lift their heads from their pillowy paws but when they register it's me, they go back to counting flies. I walk through the corridor, heading for my grandmother's room where I find her typing away on her keyboard with only one hand, the other holding a magnifying glass. I knock on the threshold so as not to startle her but she jolts all the same.

'*Hallo Oma*,' I sing-song. 'I'm back.'

She spins on her chair to face me. '*Mein spatz*, good to see you! How's Ian?'

'Good, good. Finally talked to his girlfriend-not-girlfriend.'

She puts the magnifying glass aside. 'And?'

'They're good.'

A smile starts to form across her thin lips. 'You don't like her.'

'She's not good for him.'

She barely has eyebrows but she still manages to cock one up just to mess with me. 'You've never liked Ian's girlfriends.'

'It's not what you think, okay?' Everybody in my family, including my Oma, have always harboured hopes that Ian and I would end up together at some point. I did too. Once. But not anymore.

She raises her arms in surrender. 'Then what is it?'

My shoulders slump. I stay quiet for a beat before stepping inside her room and perching on her bed. 'It's been a year and she hasn't told him that she loves him.'

She does a double take. I stare back, clueless. When she realises that's it, there's no more to the story, she throws her head back in laughter. Her giggles start as a wave, bubbly and booming through the room. It's so contagious I can't possibly be mad at her – even when I'm the butt of the joke. When she stops for air, her face is flushed, her button nose looking like a cherry tomato.

'*Ah meine kleine*,' she clasps her hands. 'You know, your Opa never told me he loved me.'

If jaws could actually drop to the floor, mine would be shattered all over this carpet. 'B– but– but– weren't you married for like, fifty years or something?'

'Forty-seven,' she corrects, her tone solemn.

'It's not like he didn't have the time to do it.'

All she does is chuckle at me as I stare at her and exhale exasperatedly. I knew their story wasn't the most romantic, I mean, he didn't even propose to her properly. According to her memory, she *thinks* they were in the middle of a make-out session – you can imagine how traumatising that was for me to hear – when he pulled away to say something along the lines of, "we should probably get married sometime soon."

'I never doubted,' she resumes. 'His love, I mean. Not even for a second. Maybe if he had been my first husband when I was young and insecure. But with your Opa–' a puff of air comes out of her wrinkly lips, her eyes becoming cloudy with all the memories I imagine are taking over her mind. 'He never faltered. I was a single mother of four, one of them sick and dying, in my late thirties and he still wanted me. He was a young ex-soldier, with his life still ahead of him but he took it. The whole package.'

Immediately the memory of my grandpa pops into my mind. His small eyes, all but consumed by his droopy lids and wrinkly skin. They were kind and soft regardless of all the horror he'd seen in life. The image of his very thin lips curved into an ever-present small smile is also very vividly ingrained in my head, again, contrasting to the huge mountain of a man he was. Now that I think about it, I can't remember his voice. I rummage through my brain, through every hidden file but come out empty-handed.

I know he had a deep, rumbling voice but that's an assumption based purely on logic. From all the stories I've heard – most of them I was told at least two times – almost none mention his voice. There aren't any anecdotes of him bellowing and roaring at anybody, but there is the infamous one when he hugged a family friend so hard that one of her ribs cracked. Funnily enough, I've heard many a mention of his laughter. A timid, throaty sound kind of like Muttley's from *Wacky Races*.

'He wasn't much of a talker, was he?' I ask Oma.

'Oh no,' she chuckles fondly. 'He never had the space to be, so he never learned how to.'

If my grandfather was a small presence in a large body, his mother was the exact opposite. Omami was a petite, lanky woman with the guts to stab Goebbels, the Nazi Minister of Propaganda, in the chest and demand he freed her husband who'd been unfairly arrested. She was the kind of woman who made demands. And people tended to it, including – and most obviously – her kids.

Opa was the youngest of three, the little boy among two girls. They were eloquent, articulate, excelled in maths and literature and history. He was dyslexic and understood what plants required to flourish. They made themselves heard, fighting for their mother's attention, drowning him out in the process. He did make himself heard some times, when it really mattered.

As a young man in 1940's Europe, he was forced to enlist in the army. But unlike most young men in 1940's Europe, a lot of Opa's time in the army was spent in solitary being punished for his impertinence. He questioned his superiors repeatedly, disagreeing with their views and because of this, Opa was considered someone who had no respect for hierarchy. A trait I supposedly inherited.

'He wrote it to me.' I frown, not following her. 'He wrote to me that he loved me once.' Oma pauses to smile probably having seen a hopeful glint in my eyes reverberating from the leap my heart gave inside my chest. 'You know he had a tremor, right? Yeah. It got bad quickly and it took a toll on him. It was really hard on him, it made him feel really embarrassed. It brought him back to his childhood, I think. But there's a reason why I'm telling you this. At that time, he was giving a different medication a try. It'd been prescribed by a new hot-shot doctor and it was pretty much a last attempt. He was giving up, my George. I'd forced him to see this doctor and the minute I set the appointment I regretted it. But I couldn't just watch him give up, could I? It was worth it though. My pushing was worth it even if it didn't last long.'

She looks away, her breath hitching and that's when it hits me. Like a lightning rushing up my spine, I realise that she never said she loved him either. To him, I'm sure she did, but not to us, not using those exact trio of words. She never needed to; it was obvious. Her love was just there, a palpable presence anytime anyone mentioned his name.

It always bummed me that there wasn't an epic love story in my family. Maybe in a twisted way my mum had a love that was one of a kind. Her first love was a charming white-collar criminal – and no, she hadn't known it when they met – that tried to steal our family's farm and threatened to run her over with a tractor. It's epic I suppose, but not the kind of love story you want for anybody, let alone your own mother. The one time I had the guts to ask if she'd ever truly loved my father she didn't hesitate. Although the word came out in a tired exhale, I heard it loud and clear. No. She never admired him or felt that passion that sweeps you off your feet. He was just there.

Oma and Opa also didn't have a love story that included The-Notebook-worthy kisses in the rain. Their love was sort of like stew, it stirred under low fire, consistent, reliable.

And I guess I've been taking it for granted.

'It'd been a week since he took the first pill, I think. But one day it worked. Just like that.' Oma snaps her fingers. 'It was a miracle. I can see him in front of me now staring at his own hands, bewildered, completely and utterly mind boggled. They'd stopped shaking, stood still like normal hands are supposed to. Immediately I started fumbling around for a pen and paper, sliding it towards him across the table. "Can you write?" I asked. He rushed to grab them and scribbled three words on the piece of paper. *Ich liebe dich.* He didn't falter, he didn't hesitate. Those were the first words your Opa could think of. Ich liebe dich.'

She meets my eyes, a content smile dancing on her lips, not a word left to say.

And I finally understand Ian.

The Stuff of Fearless Dreams
Hart Vetter

Titillation and horror make great movies.

That can be awkward, as a kid, watching with your parents.

I was twelve. Picture this: Living room, TV was still a novelty and movies were a shared experience. The whole family was watching – mom, dad, my older brother, (a jock), and me. I don't remember the title of the film. This particular scene popped up halfway through and has stayed with me to this day. There was this heavenly bevy of naked young men lined up in the back of the frame, predominant rear views and, I swear, a frontal here and there, mostly there, in the background. What an eye-opener. This was Europe, after all, where sensual realism was a thing, and, when in doubt – nude always beats prude.

The family seemed uneasy. Next, the male lead was in a medium close-up, unclothed, the navel-up kind, most appealing. His face nervous, switching to indignantly appalled when he was asked to bend over, and some white-coated doctor-guy appeared to stare right up his butt. My mouth went agape as the rest of the family kept looking stoically at the little black and white screen. It was quiet.

The movie continued on. *Leave it alone*, this inner voice of mine interjected, but I went against it and dared, timidly, 'What was that?'

Dad stirred in his favourite chair, 'That's what they do,' he said as if describing a routine as conventional as a nurse checking your pulse, 'to make sure everything's okay.'

My brother rolled his eyes, kind of embarrassed, and Mom kept her eyes glued on the TV.

From a school buddy, I learned they were figuring out who among the guys was a homo – and if you were, you'd not get drafted. Because you were a sissy, inferior, unacceptable. *Rejectable*, this inner voice of mine interpreted. I'd grown used to hearing it, just me, in my head, from an early age. What prompted this voice, I didn't know. Was it my conscience speaking up or my own inner secret pal and confidante? I was just twelve, so early age meant five. It was a voice of doubt. Who I was. That I wasn't all I was cracked up to be. *You are one of those*, the voice alluded. And it kept insisting: *Better shut up about it, keep it to yourself.* I never talked back to the voice, because that would seem crazy. And I certainly wasn't crazy. Falling asleep meant clobbering uneasy thoughts about who I was into exhaustion on many a night.

At twelve I had hoped I'd still outgrow it. Shutting up about things was smart thinking. My brother was four years older and of no help. I adored him with his youth soccer championships. For all I knew he'd probably try toughening me up in what he'd figure was a brotherly, loving way, and needle me endlessly when no one was around.

The other question gnawing in the back of my mind, disturbing and bewildering: what was it they were looking to find up a young man's behind? Was it an engraved, permanent marker identifying my kind, placed in a most discreet, awkward spot by Mother Nature herself? I never found the nerve to ask anybody and didn't know where to look it up.

I was just a naive kid, not blessed with a wealth of imagination as to the different avenues lust and desire might find to explore.

The voice kept fading over the years, even as the notion lost steam that it would just be a phase. Straight pretending was my strategy. I was twenty when the dreaded moment of my physical arrived. And the night before, the voice was back, loud and clear, messing with my head, *Guess what – your whole life is about to explode in yours and everybody's faces!* I was tossing and agonising.

The room had high ceilings and lights which were too bright. They'd gathered about thirty of us at a time for the medical exam. I was anxious, but aimed for laissez-faire while I felt my pulse racing in a mad gallop through my veins that I feared would skew my checkup data. At some point each one of us was asked to pull down his shorts and bend forward. It was for seconds only. A non-event. A prostate exam, by comparison, would be seismic.

'No haemorrhoids, that's good,' some medic said quickly, with a wink. Insufficient scrutiny to adequately diagnose anything, I thought, figuring it was just a placeholder or euphemism.

That same old law, called 'Paragraph 175', was still on the books. My knowledge about it was vague at the time, something about pink triangles and concentration camps during the country's darkest days of pure evil. Mercifully now, there seemed no appetite to go out of their way to identify and separate.

Bottom line, by implication: I was now certified to be the non-gay variety, and the authorities were evidently not about to speed up my coming-out. It left the voice speechless.

Air Force. Three tough months of basic training. I was blessed with a boring demeanour that blended in. When digging deep I knew I could locate and tap some needed butch-it-up tenacity. Frequent muscle aches and sore feet from marching 10k in rigid, unforgiving boots. A good night's rest could never be taken for granted. We had night alarms to ready ourselves within a minute, G-3 guns over the shoulders, assembling in formation, then trekking through the valley up the hill to guard the Radar Ground Control Bunker. Where my regular job in coming months was to be that of a tracker to ID commercial and other air traffic, and watching out for possible airspace violations on the dreaded East German border.

Life on base soon followed a routine which saw people leaving for home on most weekends and arriving back late on Sundays.

There were five of us in our room. Two of the recruits were quite decent looking, one of which was an older student type. There was a farm boy, big-pawed, borderline pudgy but cute, the last one was totally hot.

Don't look, the voice reemerged.

That first night in the barracks, as we were getting ready for the bunks, the hot one, an athletic, tough guy, strutted around the room in the buff for a minute chatting about one conquest or another. *Just act all cool and casual,* the voice cautioned. There was a punk side to him, I felt, a little rough around the edges. A dash of danger perhaps. Not the kind of guy I'd normally hang out with, but a brazen joy to the so-inclined eye. He reluctantly slid on a pair of the loathed, white, air force-provided undershorts. He next goaded the farm boy into pushups on the floor to prove who was the fittest. They totally went at it, neither inclined to cave. Eventually, the student cut in to give them an out, 'Guys, come on, call it a night! They're going to get us fucking exhausted soon enough at this joint. I bet as early as tomorrow.' Wheezing and winded, the warriors in their underwear climbed into their respective bunks.

No-one in our room was bashful. Physique in its prime was a beautiful thing. That voice knew when to shut up. I let the visuals take over and enjoyed the scene as a silent, appreciative observer. I developed a casual, reflexive habit of absorbing the sights.

In the mornings, we would all head down the hallway to the lavatories and showers. One recruit from another room I spotted traversing totally naked, in flip flops, towel over his shoulder, toiletries in hand, along the long corridor. I could never do that because signs of arousal would not have been an acceptable option, except just as you got out of bed first thing from whatever had fired up your dreams. Some of the guys, emerging from the showers, wet-shaved at the sinks that were set up six in a row. The vain ones worked their faces, shaving, shifting and bending toward the mirrors, often unencumbered by stitches of clothing.

It was just a crop of visuals springing up like wildflowers of raw beauty dotting a rugged landscape interspersed with thorns and thistles. Be still my foolish voice.

One late Friday afternoon at the little train station, ready for home. Track 2. The whistle went off. With just seconds to spare I climbed the extended metal steps of the second to last passenger car, with the train slowly jostling into motion. A guy came racing up the last few steps, panting for air, onto the platform, in one hand a duffle bag. They weren't going to stop for anybody. I pried my foot down to force the auto-closing door open and metal steps out, as he hopped on board through the narrowing gap right while the train was winning the upper hand grinding into forward momentum. The doors expanded for a moment, then clunked shut, with what sounded like limb-chopping force.

He sported an infectious smile. 'Good,' he gasped, 'one thing I hate is waiting.' We plunked down in an empty compartment. He was huffing. His skin was a golden shade of brown, he had big brown eyes, thick eyebrows, dark short brown hair, pronounced nose, bulging Adam's apple, thin lips, wiry, skinny. 'The fucking sadists dragged out our room inspection,' he explained. The usual shenanigans before granting weekend leave. 'The clothes in my locker weren't folded neat enough,' he shrieked, 'Fuckers! They looked hard, and found three specks of lint on the floor, so we had to mop all over again.'

He'd be getting off the train in thirty minutes, he said, for his connection. He promptly unbuttoned his fatigues, dropping them, revealing netted underwear with a pouch of fabric that housed the centre piece whose uncircumcised contours were tightly embraced by the most sensitive cloth like a delicate mould vividly capturing not just veins, but all there was. I was such a pro by now, internally breathless, successfully feigning a bored nonchalance. His undershirt off, his tanned skin tight, displaying a sinewy hint of muscles. A delicate, narrow trail of shimmering black hair migrating from belly button down. Jabbering about his girlfriend and their weekend plans, as he extracted a pair of jeans from his duffle bag, stepped in, and slowly wiggled it to his midsection. Rummaging with his hand behind and below the zipper area, until the landscape seemed fluffed and comfortable. Putting on a colourful top, and shoving his military wear into the bag that seemed filled with other dirty clothes. The passenger car kept rumbling along. I said a prompt now and then. Reaching his stop, we waved goodbye.

The camaraderie of fellow airmen was relaxed and freeing. For me, acting had long become second nature, out of self-preservation and quiet appreciation. It was the stuff that fearless dreams were made of. The unbearable sweetness of basic training.

Decades later now at get-togethers, if a conversation happened to waft toward soldiers or military service I might have let it slip that I was once a Corporal in the *Luftwaffe*. It would draw a bewildered look and a chuckle, here in the New World. At a barbecue with some fellow gays, I was trying to keep things light and sexy and mentioned to a friend my discreet viewing pleasures back in the days.

Taken aback, he said, 'Quite a creepy thing...'

Somebody else chimed in, 'Yeah, really! Bad Corporal!'

'Weren't you a band of brothers, man?'

They made it sound like I had committed incest.

Maybe they were just messing with me. I started waffling, 'We were young, thrown together for the draft from all walks... it's just that I couldn't help noticing... things...'

A woman friend wrinkled her nose, 'Very Peeping Tom-my of you!'

Damn political correctness. Damn damnation via hindsight, I thought, shrugging. 'The guys knew they looked hot. Who was I to disagree?'

My friends stared openmouthed as if my argument sucked.

My inner voice admonished, *Just shut the hell up.*

Deeds Not Words

Lisa Williams

The women weren't heard when they asked. So they smashed windows to make a din. Emily wasn't listened to when she shouted and died trying to tie a scarf to the King's Horse.

With their words ignored they planted bombs with hairpins in, at the bank hoping the explosions might attract some attention; burned VOTES FOR WOMEN in the grass at golf courses; took an axe to Wellington's Portrait in The National Gallery hoping someone might then take heed.

Not one person heard Evaline from Prison when she was the first of many to have food forced into every hole.

Contributors

Carl Alexandersson (he/him) is a queer poet based in Glasgow. He was selected for the BBC *Words First* programme in 2021, Highly Commended for the Edwin Morgan Poetry Award 2022, and a runner-up for the Grierson Verse Prize 2022. His work appears in *Atrium, Ink Sweat & Tears*, and more. His debut poetry pamphlet is forthcoming with Stewed Rhubarb Press in 2023. When not writing, he is either reading books or buying books, which are, indeed, two separate hobbies.

Shrien Alshabasy (she/her/hers) is a first generation Egyptian-American based out of New York City. She is an advocate for literacy equity and a communications specialist for higher education institutions and philanthropic organizations. Her creative writing centers on the concept of memory, hope after loss, and the voice's power in untangling shame. She writes poetry, young adult fantasy, and short stories. She has been published in *Generations Journal, Chronogram Magazine, Her Agenda, Huffington Post*, and the SUNY Open Access Repository.

Drew Boulton (she/her) is a contemporary fiction writer and poet from York. She is previously unpublished. Recently she has started petsitting for various people in her life, and so far has only lost one cat.

Carole Bromley (she/her) is a York-based poet writing for both adults and children. Published in *The Poetry Review, Rialto, The North* etc., she has three collections with Smith/Doorstop and one with Valley Press. The theme of 'voices' appealed as she is finding it increasingly hard to hear voices, hence the poem 'Subtitles' which is, sadly, entirely true!

Cat Caie (she/her), a poet and freelance music journalist based in Sheffield, has previously had her poetry published by *Dreich*, Science Museum Group on National Poetry Day and *Bloom Magazine*. The theme of voices resonated with her because of her interest in cultural identity, which she is researching for her Master's dissertation in Librarianship. Her favourite poets are Kate Baer, Helen Mort and Ada Limón.

Tinamarie Cox (she/her) lives in Arizona, USA with her husband and two children. Her poetry and prose have appeared in several publications including *Dollar Store Magazine*, *The Sirens Call*, *Red Weather*, and *Spare Parts Lit*. Her first chapbook, *Self-Destruction in Small Doses*, was recently released with Bottlecap Press. She is currently working on a second poetry collection.

Steve Denehan (he/him) lives in Kildare, Ireland with his wife Eimear and daughter Robin. He is the author of two chapbooks and four poetry collections. Winner of the Anthony Cronin Poetry Award and twice winner of *Irish Times'* New Irish Writing, his numerous publication credits include *Poetry Ireland Review* and *Westerly*. He listens to music all day long.

Jeremy Dixon (he/him) lives close to the East Yorkshire Coast, where he works part-time as a builder. His fiction has been published in the *Glittery Literary Anthology Four*, and online with *Sky Island Journal* and *Loft*. He has another piece appearing soon in *The Mocking Owl Roost*. His story was written in a bookshop–coffee shop, in the centre of York.

Ron Hardwick (he/him), a Geordie now living in East Lothian, has written short fiction for a long time. Ron has a Business Studies degree from Northumbria University and Master of Arts degrees in both Literature and Creative Writing from the Open University. Ron's work has recently been published by *Secret Attic*, *Fictionette*, *Makarelle*, *Write Time*, Leicester Charities, *Fission*, *Pure Slush* and *Cranked Anvil*. Ron still seeks a publisher for his 29 Mr Lemon private detective comic short stories!

Mark Andrew Heathcote (he/him) is adult learning difficulties support worker. He has poems published in journals, magazines, and many anthologies both online and in print. He resides in the UK and is from Manchester. His other interests include gardening, music and art. He claims to have had a somewhat poor education but tries to improve with every written word he writes. Mark is the author of *In Perpetuity* and *Back on Earth*, two books of poems published by Creative Talents Unleashed. As far as future projects go it is just to continue publishing in journals and magazines, and anthologies for now.

Christina Hennemann (she/her) is a poet and prose writer based in Ireland. Her debut poetry pamphlet was published by Sunday Mornings at the River in 2022. She won the Luain Press Poetry Competition, was shortlisted in the Anthology Poetry Award and longlisted in the National Poetry Competition. Her work appears in *The Moth*, fifth wheel, *Ink Sweat & Tears, Moria, Skylight 47*, National Poetry Month Canada, and elsewhere. She is currently working on a full-length poetry collection.

Kenneth Hickey (he/him) was born in 1975 in Cobh, Co. Cork Ireland. His work has been published in *Southword, Crannóg, THE SHOp, A New Ulster, Aesthetica Magazine* and *The Great American Poetry Show*. He was shortlisted for the Bournemouth Poetry Prize in 2022. He has been selected for the Poetry in the Park project and has been awarded a poetry mentorship by Munster Literature Centre. His debut collection *The Unicycle Paradox* was published by Revival Press in November 2021.

Tyson Higel (he/him) began writing poetry in search of fluent self-expression, something he struggles with as a person who stutters. It's on the page that he's found his voice, and his poems have appeared in the pages of the *Kings River Review, redrosethorns*, and *Corridor*, a publication local to Bellingham, WA where he lives. His chapbook *Confessions of a Stutterer* (Finishing Line Press) is forthcoming later this year.

Iqbal Hussain (he/him/his), from London, has been writing since he could hold a pencil. In 2022, he won first prize for Writing Magazine's Grand Flash competition. His work appears in various anthologies, including *Lancashire Stories* by Lancashire Libraries and *Inkandescent* by Mainstream. His story, 'A Home from Home', won Gold in the Creative Future Writers' Awards 2019. Iqbal is currently working on his debut novel, *Northern Boy*. In his teens, Iqbal appeared on *Blockbusters, Countdown* and *The Crystal Maze*.

Erin Hutchings (she/her) is from Berkshire, but is currently studying psychology at the University of Lincoln. This is her first published work, though she has been writing poetry as a hobby for many years. She has always felt passionate about social issues, and felt prompted to write this poem about the mistreatment and silencing of victims of sexual abuse.

Jen If (she/her) is a writer from the South of England published in literary magazines including *Streetcake, Déraciné, Caustic Frolic* and Flight of the Dragonfly. She writes poetry and prose from life, having lived an unusually eventful life. She mostly likes writing and walking her dogs; three Irish wolfhounds, a Doberman pinscher and one young Rottweiler. Twitter: @WriterJenIf, Instagram: @Writer_Jen_If

LJ Ireton (she/her/hers) is a poet and bookseller from London. She has a first-class BA Honours in English Language and Literature. Her poems have been published by numerous journals including: Green Ink Poetry, *The Madrigal, Spellbinder Magazine, Drawn to the Light Press, Acropolis Journal* and *Amphibian Literary*. In October 2022 her work was published in the poetry anthology *Spectrum* by Renard Press. She is fascinated by the life and lost voices of medieval and Renaissance queens, which influences much of her poetry and inspired this *York Literary Review* poem.

Zeke Jarvis (he/him/his) lives in central Illinois. His work has appeared in *Bat City Review, Moon City Review*, and *Posit*, among other places. His books include *So Anyway..., In A Family Way, The Three of Them* and *Antisocial Norms*. His favourite things to do are to play with his granddaughter and write biographical information about himself.

Emily Jayne (she/her) is an ecofeminist, poet and writer, based in York. Her previous works include contributions to the *Beyond the Walls* anthology in 2020 and 2021, a self-published poetry collection *Love on Reflection* in 2021, and a poem included in the *York Literary Review* in 2022. She recently constructed a birdfeeder, as part of her newfound interests in gardening, but so far has only seen pigeons and a few cats enjoying her efforts.

Anita John (she/her) hails from Sheffield and lives in Scotland. She's published in *Aesthetica Magazine, MsLexia, New Writing Scotland, Gutter, The High Window, Northwords Now, PENning, The Scotsman* and other magazines. She writes short scripts and poetry, is a founding member of Borders Pub Theatre, and a member of the poetry and piano trio Contrappuntistica. Nature, family and voices from the past constantly find their way into her work so she loved this theme! See: anitajohn.co.uk

Dana Knott (she/her) works as a library director in Columbus, Ohio, and edits *tiny wren lit*. Voice emerged as a central theme in her collection on Pre-Raphaelite artist, poet, and model Elizabeth Siddal. These poems attempt to push past the salacious details of Siddal's life – her relationship with Rossetti, her addiction, and her exhumation – to center her voice. Find some of Dana's Lizzie poems in *Ethel* zine, *Dodging the Rain, FERAL*, Green Ink Poetry, *Trouvaille Review*, and *The Orchards Poetry Journal*.

Grace Laidler (she/her) is a first-year student, studying film and television production. She currently lives in York, but is originally from South Shields. Grace has always loved creative writing and has recently performed a short story at the York Literature Festival. In her spare time, she is a regular contributor to *The Film Magazine* and *True Faith: Newcastle United Fanzine*. Her go-to karaoke song is Carly Simon's 'You're So Vain'.

Alan McKean (he/him) is a retired Clog Morris dancer living in Lancashire, he has been writing for around twenty years, about what he sees and hears around him, and tries to paint pictures with words, instead of brushes. For nearly sixty years, he has held a strong interest in dialect poetry, from the nineteenth century poets to modern day equivalents, as he thinks their vocabulary adds life, vibrancy, and often humour to their voice, even in their darkest times.

Debasish Mishra (he/his) is a Senior Research Fellow at National Institute of Science Education and Research, HBNI, India. He is the recipient of the 2019 Bharat Award for Literature and the 2017 Reuel International Best Upcoming Poet Prize. His recent poems have appeared in *North Dakota Quarterly*, *Penumbra*, *California Quarterly*, *Rubbertop Review*, *Perceptions*, *Apricity*, *Hawai'i Pacific Review*, and elsewhere. His first book *Lost in Obscurity and Other Stories* was recently published by Book Street Publications in 2022.

Quinn Murphy (she/her) is an 18-year-old writer based in British Columbia, Canada. Her poems have been published in the *Blue Marble Review*, *Ice Lolly Review*, and *Spiritus Mundi Review*. Her work has also appeared in *Spellbinder Magazine*, where her poem *A Dragon Curled Around My Heart* was chosen as an Editor's Pick for the Winter 2023 issue. She has a passion for creative writing, and she hopes to publish a novel one day.

Originally from Middlesbrough, **E.R. Murray** (she/her) lives in rural Ireland, where she grows vegetables, catches mackerel, and hikes in the rain. Her novels include *Caramel Hearts* and the award-winning Nine Lives Trilogy: *The Book of Learning* (Dublin UNESCO Citywide Read 2016), *The Book of Shadows* (shortlisted Irish Literacy Association Award & Irish Book Awards), and *The Book of Revenge*. Recent anthology/journal publications include *Women on Nature*, *Ponder Review*, *Paper Lanterns*, *Terrain*, *Not Very Quiet*, *Popshot*, *Banshee*, and *Ropes*. Twitter: @ERMurray

June O'Sullivan (she/her) lives on an island in Co. Kerry, Ireland. She is submitting her first novel, writing her second and writes flash fiction and short stories. She has been published in the *Leicester Writes Short Story Prize* 2022 and *The Ogham Stone Journal* (Uni of Limerick). She is a student of the MA in Creative Writing at the University of Limerick and she wrote this piece as a creative response to a module on Holocaust literature.

Briá Purdy (she/her) is a writer and artist based in Manchester. Her poetry has been published in *Popshot*. She is the founder of *The Head of a Woman*, a multilingual arts and culture zine inspired by her love for surrealist imagery and theoretical physics. Briá is currently teaching art classes and is working on a novel about love, death, and Proust. She usually wears red.

S. Reeson (she/they) is 56 and bisexual. They have been published by Green Ink Poetry, *Acropolis Journal, Selcouth Station, Black Bough Poetry, Paragraph Planet, Forest Arts*, Flapjack Press, *Visual Verse* and *Dreich*. In October 2022 they were shortlisted for inclusion as part of the South Bank Centre New Poets Collective. A debut poetry pamphlet entitled *Flammable Solid* was published by Flight of the Dragonfly Press in November 2022. When not being a poet they enjoy lifting heavy weights.

Bill Richardson (he/him) is Emeritus Professor in Spanish at the University of Galway, Ireland, and has re-engaged in recent years with his passion for creative writing. He enjoys swimming in the Atlantic and practising tai chi to the music of Arvo Pärt. He has had poems published in *Skylight 47, Atrium, The Seventh Quarry, Amethyst Review, The Stony Thursday Book, Orbis, The Orchards Poetry Journal, 14 Magazine, Boats Against The Current, The High Window* and the *Fish Anthology 2020*.

JY Saville (she/her) writes stories of various lengths and genres in West Yorkshire, and was shortlisted for the Comedy Women in Print Short Story prize 2022/23. Her short fiction has been published in more than forty places including *Untitled:Voices, Ellipsis Zine*, and *Confingo*. She tweets @JYSaville and spends more time than is healthy researching family history.

Nileena Sunil (she/her) lives in India. She has works published in *Borderless Journal, Kitaab, Tales from an Unfamiliar Nation, Setu* and *The Chakkar*, as well as the anthologies *The Collapsar Directive* and

Flash Fiction Addiction. She has a deep and abiding love for anything to do with books and writing.

Karoline Tübben (she/her) is a queer, German/Latina writer with an International Relations degree she'll probably never use. She worked as a translator and junior editor for the International Relations Office at Belo Horizonte City Hall before moving to the U K to study Publishing and Creative Writing. Now she's a bartender – a job she swears she got just for the buckets of money she gets every month, not because of all the stories she overhears from behind the bar.

Hart Vetter (he/him) switched from longer tales to short stories in 2021. Newly retired. Forever writer. Immigrant. Queer. Divorced. Dad. Devoted dog walker in the Hudson Rivertown of Nyack, NY. Recent work appeared or is slated in *Literary Heist*, *The Write Launch*, *The Wild Word*, *Flash Fiction Magazine*, and elsewhere. *York Literary Review*'s theme of Voices 'spoke' to him, conjuring up that powerful inner one, that can wield influence over what we do, for better or worse, and miraculously propel our creative spirits.

Lisa Williams (she/her) is a writer from Leicester. She has a Masters in Creative Writing from Leicester University and tends to write mostly short fiction. Her work has been published widely online and most recently in anthologies from Red Polka Books, Kobayaashi Studios and Chapeltown Books. As soon as she heard about the voices theme she knew she wanted to write about the suffragettes and to work to a word limit; 'Deeds not Words' is exactly one hundred words. You can find her online @noodleBubble.

www.ingramcontent.com/pod-product-compliance
Lightning Source LLC
Chambersburg PA
CBHW050904180626
46814CB00007B/2891